THE LAST KIDS ON EARTH

THRILLING TALES FROM THE TREE HOUSE

THE LAST KIDS ON EARTH

THRILLING TALES FROM THE TREE HOUSE

With illustrations by DOUGLAS HOLGATE,
Lorena Alvarez Gómez, Xavier Bonet,
Jay Cooper, Christopher Mitten,
and Anoosha Syed

Farshore

First published in the United States of America by Viking,
An imprint of Penguin Random House LLC, 2021

This edition published in 2021 by Farshore

An imprint of HarperCollins*Publishers*
1 London Bridge Street, London SE1 9GF

farshore.co.uk

HarperCollins*Publishers*
1st Floor, Watermarque Building,
Ringsend Road, Dublin 4, Ireland

ISBN 978 0 0084 8587 0
Printed in the UK by Bell & Bain Ltd, Glasgow
1

A CIP catalogue record for this title is available from the British Library

For Alyse. —M. B.

To the Grundy Outlaws: Angus, Syd, Noah, Jak, Jake, Flynn, and Hamish. Do it for Silverwings. Do it for Phil, and do it for the gang! —D. H.

CONTENTS

Midnight parties are the best parties!
Ain't no party like a midnight party 'cause a midnight party happens LATE.
Delicious marshmallow pies coming out of the Easy-Bake!
I AM READY TO SLICE THEM!
String lights on full blast!
All eleven speakers at maximum volume! Party music is going!
Board games are ready to go!
Wait. Did you guys hear that?

CRASH! SMASH!
GRAWWR!
Does anyonc see it?
Uh, yup. And it sees us.
I really wish we had curtains.
Hey, I offered to sew curtains! But Jack said curtains are for old people!
No. I said curtains **remind** me of old people.

This is bad. It appears we are trapped.
NO, WE ARE NOT TRAPPED. BECAUSE I AM BRAVE. I WILL FIGHT THE BEAST. ALONE.
Nope. Sorry, Skaelka. Can't let you have all the glory. I'm gonna pummel this dude Savage-style. As in— no help needed.
This is rash, but I AM eager to test out my new Monster-B-Gone cannon.
So . . . I will face the monster!
No way! I called facing the beast alone first . . .
ON MY OWN! LIKE A WORTHY SOLO HERO DUDE!
Guys . . . HELLO! We can't ALL battle the monster solo. The whole point of solo is that it's done—y'know— solo.
THEN WHOEVER IS MOST WORTHY SHALL BATTLE THE MONSTER. AND THAT IS ME! MY AXE HAS FELLED MANY BEASTS!

I battled a hundred zombies during the Battle of the Hundred Zombies!
CENSORED
You don't want to know the things I've done.
BOOM
BOOM
BOOM
BOOM
My Slicer destroyed Blarg! I've spilled more neon slime than Nickelodeon Studios!
Blasty helped me take down a whole family of Ploonks!
My zapping gadget thwarted that fur creature!

This is gonna be tough . . .
Yeah, we all have awesome monster and zombie battling stories . . .
That's it! STORIES! A story-off. Whoever's story proves them MOST WORTHY wins! And gets to—y'know—battle the big monster. El solo style.
That's just dumb.
Eek!
CLUTCH
OK, fine . . . only so we can get this over with.
LET GO OF DIRK, you multiple-fisted meanie!

Not too many minutes later . . .
Let's make it quick. Don't know how long the tree house can hold out.
NOT I. SKAELKA WILL WAIT TO HEAR YOUR SUBPAR TALES—THEN DEMOLISH THEM WITH MY OWN!
So, who's going first?
Why don't we get the best story out of the way now—that way, you guys'll know what you're up against. So, batter up . . .
That means I'm going first. Just in case it wasn't clear. Was it clear? It was clear, right?
Yes, Jack, it was clear.

SWINGIN' JACK SULLIVAN & THE GOOD NEWS BUDDIES IN . . .

DANGER ON THE DIAMOND!

BOOM! GRAND SLAM! It's a walk-off, it's a walk-off. . . .

Another game of Sgt. Baseball's Home Run Slaughter—and another victory for Team Quack. QUACK! QUACK!

Your team name is dumb.

That was bunk! I had the sun in my eyes!

story by Max Brallier art by Xavier Bonet

Whoa, the sun's up?

Have we been playing all night?

It is easy to lose track of time during the apocalypse, friend . . .

Sonic screwdrivers—that **reminds** me! **Guys!** You know what today is?

JUMP!

It's opening day! First day of baseball season!
Or it would be, if, y'know...
Quint, wait, you like sports?
I don't like sports, plural. I like **sport**. BASEBALL. Scorekeeping, advanced statistics, the infield-outfield double-double-triple shift. Ahh. Glorious. . . .
SLAM!
SHAKE!
Uh-oh! The monsters are getting rambunctious again!
THONK!
THONK!
THONK!
It's too early, Thronn!
HSSS! BUT I'M THSO BORED!!

MONSTERS BEHAVING HORRIBLY MONTAGE!

KRUNCH!
WHACK!
SHATTER!

WHEE! WHIMSY!
Don't chop me in half! I contain multitudes! LITERALLY!

SQUIRM, SQUIRM
NO, BIGGUN! NO MORE FLINGING!
It's like they've gone too long without exercise. I know how I get—
OOH!
Quint's sad longing for baseball season gives me an idea!
A brilliant idea that will stop these monsters from behaving horribly.
We're gonna play baseball.

Moments later . . .
Yoohoo! Hi! You guys wanna play a game?
RING RING!
GAME? IS IT FAST-PACED AND VIOLENT?
Not that violent.
It's the **slowest**.
But it's our great pastime!
AFTER THE GAME IS DONE, WILL THERE BE A GREAT SACRIFICE?
Even better! After the game, there will be a great . . . **PIZZA PARTY!**
As is tradition!
WOOOO!
Yippee!
WOOO!

Ninety-seven minutes later . . .
Now, I'll be the gruff-but-lovable coach who whips you bums into shape. And you guys—well, you just be you.
Is this all some sort of elaborate ploy wherein you get to live out your Sandlot, Bad News Bears, and A League of Their Own fantasies?
Perhaps. . . .
This walk is endless. Why don't we just play at the old dirt pit?
Because this is special! We're playing at the most pristine field in the county!
The one at Wakefield High . . .
It's true. I had a field hockey tournament there, and it's legit.
Y'know, it's less pristine than I remembered.
And less empty than I expected. Look!
WELL, LOOK WHO IT IS. THE JOE'S PIZZA CROWD.

STEP NO FURTHER, FLESHBUCKETS! THIS FIELD IS OURS. NOW— AND FOREVER.
Like fun it is!

CAREFUL, HUMANS. THAT'S BURKIN—AND THESE ARE THE STONEBURGERS. A BAND OF GRUMPS.
I eat bands of grumps for breakfast. . . .
You eat Teddy Grahams for breakfast, Jack. And like I told you, **that's** why you're so tired in the afternoon.

SORRY. LOOKS LIKE IT'S YOUR UNLUCKY DAY.
Ha! Shows what you know. **Every day** is my unlucky day.
Don't worry, Jack. I'LL handle this. . . .

I'm afraid you're the one who's out of luck, Burkin. Field usage requests must be filed forty-eight hours in advance, in person, at the Wakefield Parks and Community Services Centre. Now, I sure hope you filed the proper paperwork . . . or, oh boy, are you gonna look silly.
Only you can make a fight like this uncool.

BEEEEEEEELLLLLCH!

No monster—
no matter how big, how scaly, or how unconcerned with proper paperwork procedure—
is keeping us off this field.
HOW ABOUT THIS . . . ONE GAME. IF YOU WIN, THE FIELD IS YOURS. IF WE WIN, WE GET RIGHTS TO THE FIELD AND . . . SOMETHING ELSE.
Sure! Fine! Whatever it is, we're in!
Personally, I'd love to know what the "something else" is before we start agreeing to things.
Of course. Otherwise—

NOPE! DOESN'T MATTER! WHATEVER IT IS, WE'RE PLAYING. Deal?
DEAL.
Well, Jack—now that it's too late to do anything about it—I would love to know what we're playing for.
Fine, fine.

WHISPER, WHISPER
What?! . . . OUR SOULS?!?
TOMORROW. DAWN.

THE NEXT DAY. DAWN.
CRACK!
FIZZZ
GULP!
Listen up, team!
CRUNCH!
What are we gonna do?
NOT LOSE!
When are we gonna do it?
IN A FEW MINUTES!
Because when the going gets tough, the tough get going!
Which is a phrase that confuses me because "get going" means "leave" and leaving when things get tough doesn't sound very tough at all, but whatever, you get the gist!
Now, let's go out there and **show these bad guys who's who!!**
I WISH JUNE WAS COACH.
Sing it, sister.

I'll confirm, but yes, I believe we are using *Rock N' Jock* scoring.

GLOBLET! You're coaching **our rivals?!**
What?? How **could** you??
They told me I had a cool hat.

We're in a fight, Globs.
Again?
OK, everyone. It's time . . . LET'S PLAY SOME BALL!

Herman's
HOT DOG PALACE
Bonanza-Rama
Herman's
HOT DOG PALACE
Bonanza-Rama

Seventeen minutes later . . .
Well, this is not going like I'd hoped. . . .

PTUI!
WOO-HOO, TWENTY-SEVEN TASTY POINTS!

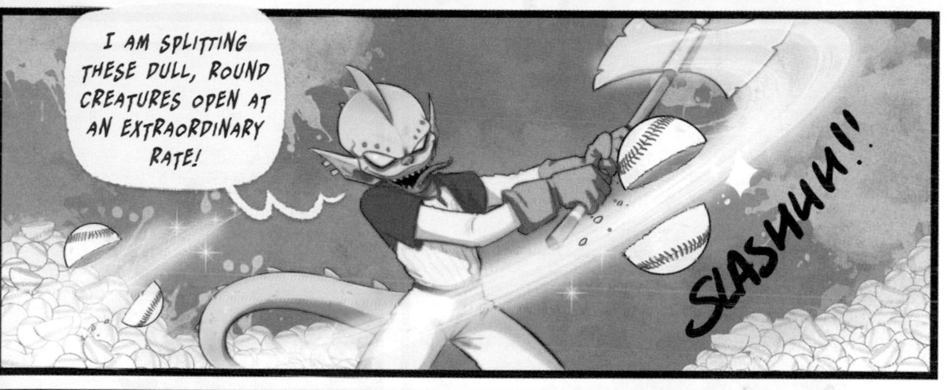
I AM SPLITTING THESE DULL, ROUND CREATURES OPEN AT AN EXTRAORDINARY RATE!
SLASHHH!!

SKREEEEEE!!!
Charge the mound, buddy!
I will not.
JOE'S PIZZA

Enough! Time! TIME-OUT!

Deal's off! This isn't baseball!
This *is* baseball. At least the way it's played in our dimension.
You sound like Johnny Steve . . . !
Gosh, I miss that owl-shaped bum.

There's no way that there's a sport called baseball in your dimension that's kind of similar with bases and balls and bats, but not identical, either.
The odds are not good.
AHH, WHAT DO YOU CARE? YOU'RE JUST SAD YOU CAN'T WIN!

Fine! We'll play your way and we'll WIN. Come on, guys. . . .

POW!

SLIDE!

This should tie it up!

Boom! Game! Catch you monster jerks on the flip-flop!
MIDNIGHT BLAST!

VICTORY!

LITTLE RUBBER ONE, YOU HAVE LET US DOWN!

LITTLE GUM WAD, YOU FAILED TO LEAD US TO VICTORY. AND FOR THAT, YOU WILL PAY . . . WITH YOUR LIFE!

SQUIRSH!

THIS IS OK! I'M FINE WITH THIS! I VOLUNTEER AS TRIBUUUUUUUUUUUTE!
PSHOOO!

Don't worry, Globlet, we're coming! I'm sorry I said we're in a fight!

Globlet, are you—
TENTACLE SURPRISE!
WHOA!

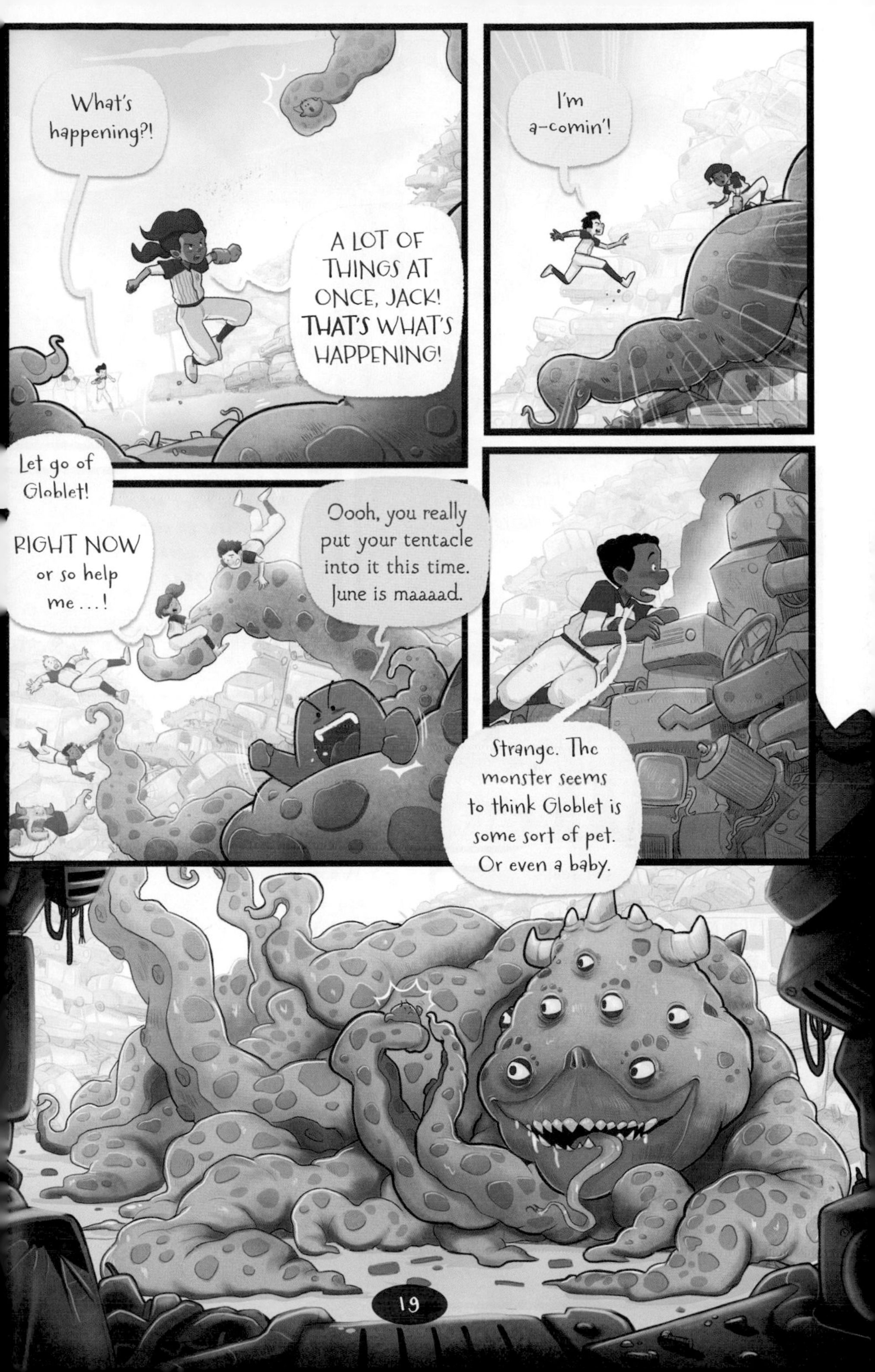
What's happening?!
A LOT OF THINGS AT ONCE, JACK! THAT'S WHAT'S HAPPENING!
I'm a-comin'!
Let go of Globlet!
RIGHT NOW or so help me . . . !
Oooh, you really put your tentacle into it this time. June is maaaad.
Strange. The monster seems to think Globlet is some sort of pet. Or even a baby.

KRAK!
SHRIEEEK!
Oof!
HAHAHA! CACKLE! CACKLE!
THAT'S THE BEASTROSITY. GOOD LUCK GETTING YOUR FRIEND BACK.
BUT WE LOST!! THAT MEANS WE DON'T GET THEIR SOLES! WE NEED THOSE—WE HAVE NO SHOES!
WE CAN STOP AT PAYLESS ON THE WAY HOME, OK? JUST RELAX.
Ohhh, soles—not souls. What a relief!
For real. Although my Light-Upz are in pretty bad shape.
Guys! Focus! Globlet's in danger!
IF GLOBLET IS STILL WITH THE BEASTROSITY BY SUNSET, SHE WILL BECOME ITS SNUGGLY FOR LIFE. BONDED FOREVER.
We gotta figure out a way to get Globlet away from that Beastrosity.
Friends . . . it's gadget time! Let's get to work. . . .

ATTEMPT #1!

FAILURE!

ATTEMPT #2!

FAILURE!
Oops!

This will **definitely** work. Just hang on tight.

FLING!

Bardle? What . . . ?

YOU PLAY FOR THE HONOUR OF JOE'S PIZZA, JACK. AND YOUR ENEMIES?

WHO DO THEY PLAY FOR?

What?
Bardle, stop talking in riddles **just once!** You're **dreamworld Bardle**—just give it to me straight!
SIGH.

FINE, JACK. THE STONEBURG MONSTERS' UNIFORMS. THINK ABOUT THEIR UNIFORMS!
Their uniforms . . . ?

Herman's Hot Dog Palace Bonanza-Rama!

Later . . .

I have come to claim my friend.
Well, more June's friend, really. I mean, we're all friends.
But Globlet and I don't hang out one-on-one much.
I just kinda think we wouldn't have that much to talk about.
But then again, maybe we would! And maybe we should hang out more! Am I just being . . .

HEEEEEEY, BEASTIE BEASTIE! SUH-WIIIING, BEASTIE!
WE NEED A PITCHER, NOT A BELLY ITCHER!
Give us back **Globlet**, why you gotta **hog her!**

NOW!

GRUNT

RAWR!
DUCK!

JUNE! I knew you would come for me!
Oh, hi, Jack.

Did you hear what I was saying? Do you think we should hang out more?
I'm good.
WALL CRUMBLE!

He didn't even use a gadget. . . .

Ooh, fun tour.
And the last stop is the ol' hot dog spot!
YES! THEY HAVE CURLY FRIES!
THE SIGN SAYS EMPLOYEES ONLY. IT'S NOT COMPLICATED!
EMPLOYEES ONLY
Official business, Chef!
HEY, WHAT THE—ARGH!
My bad, Warg!
There! My team! Oh boy, I am gonna chew them out.
We'll leave that to the Beastrosity.

HOT DOG
Bonama-Ra
Hey, Beastrosity! That monster's head looks like a fun play toy! Have at it!
LET'S GET OUTTA HERE!
A-WHA?
POW!
SLAM!

Later . . .
BASEBALL IS QUITE FUN.
Uh-oh. This next part is the worst.
PIZZA

NOOOO! NOT MY BREATHING HOLES!

AS YUGGOTH IS MY WITNESS, I WILL NEVER MESS WITH JACK SULLIVAN AGAIN! WHAT A COOL GUY. IT SEEMS LIKE HIS FRIENDS MAYBE DON'T APPRECIATE HIM AS MUCH AS THEY SHOULD.
END!

Aaaand . . . SCENE! So, do I win? Do I get to fight the monster now?
I remember that. Best day ever.
Globlet, I remember that day too—and it didn't happen like that AT ALL.
That story was about nineteen percent true.
Bro. You couldn't hit a home run if I swung the bat FOR you.
And Jack, I'm sorry—did you say you're not as appreciated as you should be? Is that what I heard, there?
Hey, I didn't say it! That jerky monster Burkin did. I don't control what he says.
I'm just relaying the facts.
SULLIVAN, THAT STORY WAS A STRING OF LIES LONGER THAN A GORLAX INTESTINE.
I'LL be nice and say "exaggerations."
Exaggerations . . . and The Sandlot.
You're killin' me, Sulls!

Next! I call next! Time for my story!
Can't be worse than Jack's "totally never happened" story.
You mean the lie-filled one filled with all the lies?
That's the one.
I liked Jack's story, 'cause I had tons of rad screen time. But not as much as I've got in THIS STORY . . .
NERDS
THIS STORY which is one hundred percent FACTUAL and TOTALLY DEFINITELY HAPPENED.
Presented for the approval of the Midnight Society . . .

WHERE'S MY CHEF'S ASSISTANT?
Did someone say . . . CHEF'S ASSISTANT??
Also, I believe the term is *sous chef.*
IIIIIIII'm baaaaaaack!
APPLAUSE
now!!!
IT'S GLOBLET! STARRING IN:
A GAGGLE of GLOBLETS
story by Max Brallier
art by Anoosha Syed
wink

Oohmygosh, Chef, you'll NEVER guess the dream I had!
Siiigh...
COURSE NOT. IT WAS YOUR DREAM, GLOB—

See, I was THE most important monster in the globosphere, and I could do **anything** I wanted, and everyone loved me. Even you! Well, everyone except . . .

MAYO!

We meet again. . . . I told you, stay out of my dreams!

YOU DONE SCOLDING THE MAYO? 'CAUSE WE GOT COOKIN' TO DO.
What's on the menu today, Cheffy Pants?
MAYO
Tie!
2 HOT 2 HANDLE

YOU, LITTLE GOO WAD, ARE ABOUT TO FIND OUT WHY *INTERDIMENSIONAL MICHELIN MAGAZINE* AWARDED ME **ZERO** GOLDEN TYRES. WE'RE MAKING THE ULTIMATE POWER SUB!

FWAP!!

I'M GONNA NEED A METRIC TON OF SHREDDED MOZZ, **EXACTLY** TWENTY-SEVEN FEET OF LIQUORICE, AAAAAND A JAR OF SAP FROM THE OL' MAPLE TREE OUT BACK.

On it, Chef-ster!
bounce!
bounce!
Mario's Mozzarella
PREMIUM ARTIFICIAL 'CHEESE'
FEEL THE BURN! SMELL THE CHERRY!
WHIP!
WHIP!
licorice
Mama Nature's finest!
A SPRINKLE OF THIS, A PINCH OF THAT, AND . . .
HEY!
WHERE'S MY FRYING PAN SIGNED BY GIL FIERI, GUY FIERI'S LESSER-KNOWN BROTHER?
That's it, Globlet.
Now give me duck face.
Now roar like a lion.
Now sneeze like a human.
Now pirouette!
hop!
SPIN!
!!!!
BUMP!

TENSE KNIFE FLIP!

SLOW-MO STYLE!

SLIIICE!
THUNK!

UH-OH!

uh-oh.

AAHHHHH!!
AAHHH!!

Bubble
Bubble
SHAAKE
SHAAAKE

POP!
Um.

POP!
POP!

GEEZ, GLOB, DID YOU KNOW YOU COULD DO THAT?
Oh yeah yeah, tooooootally . . . NOT!

Five minutes later . . .
Twinsies!!
Gah! We're gonna have SO much fun. I've always wanted a twin sis!
Let's do twin stuff . . . NOW!
!!!
WE ARE HAVING FUN!
Perfectly balanced!
Livin' that influencer lifestyle!
PEDAL
PEDAL
Welp.
That day was a doozy, now it's time for me to snoozy.
I'd invite you to stay, but my dream drawer is at capacity.
Zero vacancies!
But there's a charming bed and breakfast right up the road.
Toodles!
SLAM!

Later that night . . .

Meanwhile, at the tree house . . .
1st ANNUAL FOOD MASTER FRENZY
Thirty seconds! Jack, you'd better start plating . . .
My cherry glaze isn't ready!!

NO EXCUSES!
I had to ice this whole cake with one lousy piping bag.

TIME'S UP!!
Utensils DOWN!
RRRRIIING!!!

Meep!
Sigh.
Yeep!

OK, Rover. Winner gets a full week off of dish duty.
So choose carefully.

I swear, if my Butterfinger buttercream isn't enough to take first place . . .
bite bite!

Clearly, you've never tasted Quint's famous cinnamon-sugar ranch dip.

I can't watch! Tell me when it's over!

???
C'mon, Rover! WHO WON?!

Hey, rad! Globlet's here!

Whoa . . . is anyone else seeing— septuple?
I hate surprise guest judges . . .
<Sigh,> Don't ask.
Flop
Flop!

Nineteen zany minutes later . . .
WHY ARE THERE SO MANY GLOBLETS?
Now say ahhhhh.
No way. Get that thing away from me!
Now, Jack. Only good patients get lollipops.
Oh, hiiiii. I'm June Del Tooooro. I'm the number-one reporter in Waaaaaaaaaaaakefield, I don't need help from ANYbody!
Globletday Night LIVE!
OMG, is that me?
It is me, isn't it?
Yeah, that's **def** me.
Well, a rootin' tootin' day to y'all—I'm Dirk Savage, the Lonely Ranger. Any of you folks fancy a turnip salad from my humble garden?
It's LONE Ranger, not LONELY Ranger.
Is it, though, Dirk?
Is it?

Uh—guys? Is anyone even the least bit interested in how all this happened?
Hey, watch it, bro.
Hard to pay attention, Quint! I'm too **wrapped up** in all these Globlets!
Where'd you learn to act like that?
Oh, I picked it up at a charming bed and breakfast up the road . . .
Hey, June!
Over here! Remember! Your best bud! Girlfriends 4 lyfe?
Hhmm?
That's IT! No one steals my best friend and gets away with it!

Stay away from my BFF, ya hear?
POKE!
hop!
If she's **your** BFF, she's **my** BFF. I AM you.

NO! June and I went on a wild flight and a cool guy wrote a book about it, and *you* weren't there, and *I* was, and we had the **BEST** time, and you wouldn't know **anything** about it!
Ouch!

Oh, *wouldn't* I? Tell me, how *are* Neon and Johnny Steve these days?

<*Gasp!*> You ***MONSTER.***
OK settle down, Globlet. Or, wait . . .
Shoot, it's hard to tell you guys apart!

June, ol' buddy, ol' pal! It's **me**! Your BFF! WHAT CAN I DO TO **PROVE** IT??
Relax, Globlet. I believe you.

Oh, June. *Tsk tsk.* You just made a **globumental** mistake.
frosting

GASP!!
You know what the world needs more of?
ME!
ubble
SHAAKE
frosting
SHAAKE
Bubble
SQUEEZE!
Have fun with all the MEs, losers!!
jump!
We've got major Globlet problems.
What do we do?
cannon glob!!
We do the only thing we can do right now:
BRAINSTORM SESSION.

One hour later:
WeLL, friends, that brainstorm session was a fail.
What happens if that Evil Globlet creates even more of these things?
THINGS?? I'll have you know the Globlets are a proud species.
Globlet, you're not a species. ALL these Globlets are extensions of you.
Oh, yeah.
ZZZZ
ZZZZZ
ZZZZZ
ZZZZ

???
murmur
Does anyone hear . . . like, weird chitchat?
Don't do it, Quint! It's a trap!
We have to know what we're dealing with!
. . . ohmygosh you *DIDN'T!*
Whee!
Yay!
For the Globolution!
. . . I know, RIGHT? I mean, she could have just told me she didn't like surprise skydiving.
100
100
. . . and then I said, could you BE any more extra?
Uh, friends? I think it's time we hit the streets and survey the damage . . .

Look at all of 'em! The wonder. The majesty!
No, Jack! It's bad! The Globlets have taken over Wakefield!
Glob
Hah! Look at those humans with their weird human faces!
Wow, is that really what Globlet thinks of us?
LOL I can't believe I'm *friends* with those kids!
Only subconsciously, June! Only subconsciously!
If we don't act fast, the world will be overrun with Globlets! And after that, perhaps . . . AN ENTIRE UNIVERSE OF GLOBLETS!
You're picturing, an **actual** outer space full of Globlets right now, aren't you, Quint?
You know I am, June.
12340

linglob memorial
glob-sphinx
Statue of globerty
10000
mount globmore!!
globfel tower
glob day parade

globiter
globtune
globturn
glob black hole

There's no **way** that can happen. There's gotta be a way outta this.
Can't we just do what adults do and ignore the problem until it goes away?
Uh, I don't think this is going away anytime soon . . .
Cowabunga, Globs!
Tubular!
No. The only way to settle this is a **Glob-Off**.
evil globlet
CLENCH!
That . . . doesn't sound good.
What's a—
NO, PLEASE! FOR THE LOVE OF GLOB, ANYTHING BUT A GLOB-OFF!
I know. It's bad. REAL BAD. But somebody's gotta fight for these little Glob-smackers. And that somebody is—
ME!
No, duder. Not this time.
PULL
Irregardless . . .
Not a word.
I started this thing, and by Glob, I'm gonna finish it.
The Glob-Off will commence at dusk.

GLOB V.S GLOB

My fellow Globlets!

WooHoo!

I was once as you are! I understand your joy, your pain, your craving for a pastrami on rye with a sour pickle HOLD THE MAYO. By gosh, hold the mayo.

But you deserve to follow your dreams!

To live, laugh, love. And to hang LIVE, LAUGH, LOVE signs in your farmhouse-style kitchens!

I know a millennium is a short life span, but we gotta make the most of it!

Who's with me??

That was sweet, but can we hurry it along? I have a Settlers of Catan game at eight, and I forfeit if I'm late.

K.O.

40

GLOBLET CLASSIC

VS

EVIL GLOBLET

Work it, Globlet.

WORK IT. YOU GOT THIS. THIS IS YOUR MOMENT, AND YOU MIGHT NEVER GET IT AGAIN!

grab!

Wait . . .
WHAT? This
is a Glob-Off?
THIS??

You think
you can
take me,
hot shot?
That's right.
I am a hot shot.
And you're a
not-shot!
Wooooow.
Good one.

Three hours later . . .

How much longer?? This is worse than Jack and Quint's weekend-long *Galaxy Quest* marathon.

Hey! *Galaxy Quest* is a quality film with limitless review value. It should be watched daily, at minimum!

More like ad nauseum.

GASP!
DROP!!

NO!

Aha! YES! You are WEAK! I AM THE ONE TRUE GLOBLET. I will lead our army against the world and be its ruler for all time!
And now, the coup de grâce . . .
PRESS!
Not so fast, you cheap knock-off, wannabe, imposter, phony, fake, sham, fraud–
Think you can defeat me with synonyms?
Yep!
See, you forgot, two crucial facts. One: I ate two of Chef's subs this morning, so I've got CRAZY energy And two? Only the real Globlet can do this–
WICKED COOL SNEAK ATTACK!™
THESAURUS
CRONCH!

AAAAHHHHHHHHHH!!!
Stretch

GASP!
Wicked.

gulp!

Ah-choo!!
CLANK!

Oops! My bad.

Globlet! Globlet! Globlet! Globlet! Globlet!

Globlet, buddy, you did it!!
Go, my children!
Be free.
Frolic into the night!
Order the most expensive sushi on the menu!
DANCE LIKE NOBODY'S WATCHING! BE THE GLOB YOU WISH TO SEE IN THE WORLD.
END!

Chew on that, dweebs. Also, feel free to chew on those scattered nerds.
Yummy.
That's definitely not canon.
Not one single ounce of that story was real! That's less than canon!
QUESTION MY STORY AGAIN, HUMAN BOYS, AND I'LL BLAST YOU OUT OF A CANNON!
Just like I do every night in my fave recurring dream.

Ooh! I know what my story is gonna be!
Got my story! My turn! My turn!
QUINT'S COMICS!
I don't need to regale you orally with my tall tale. Because I shall regale you VISUALLY! It's right here. . . .
A Quint original comic book!
STARRING THE STARS OF THE STAR-STUDDED ATTACK OF THE KILLER YO-YOS! THIS SUMMER, MEET...
SUPER INVENTORIST DUDE!
SMACK!

Gather round, readers. And by readers, I'm talking to you five.
But also . . .
YOU!
You? You who?
It's meta, Jack. You wouldn't get it.
Ooh. Someone say Yoo-hoo? I'm in for imitation chocolate milk!
Know what else Jack doesn't get? My vote for best story.
YOU KNOW WHAT JACK SHOULD GET? MY AXE! TO HIS KNEECAP!

OK, settle in. Everyone, please witness . . . MY CARTOON ART!

DOC BAKER
SUPER INVENTORIST DUDE!
FEATURING SIDEKICK BOY!
Prepare yourselves for strange action, intense drama, aaaaaaaaand . . .

DOC BAKER
SUPER INVENTORIST DUDE!
Prepare yourself for Quint-drawn illustrations and Quint-scrawled dialogue . . .

SUPER INVENTORIST DUDE!
And now, without further ado, I give you . . .

THE PERNICIOUS PUTTY PREDICAMENT

~~story by Max Brallier art by Jay Cooper~~

Story and Art by QUINT BAKER

FROM THE CREATOR OF COSMIC BURGER PATROL & NINJA SPACE AVENGER IN SPACE!

STARRING THE STARS OF THE STAR-STUDDED ATTACK OF THE KILLER YO-YOS! THIS SUMMER, MEET...

SUPER INVENTORIST DUDE!

We find our heroes at home, assuming their everyday, non-hero alter egos: **Quint Baker** and **Jack Sullivan**. Mild-mannered best friends, and two of the last kids on Earth. Just another day at the tree house at the end of the world . . .

Quint, I am having the **WORST DAY!**
Uh-huh . . .
JOE'S PIZZA

And I'm feeling **extra whiny** about it!
That's no good.

First, I didn't get to sleep in late because the sun was being, like, **EXTRA SUNNY!**

Then **ALL THE DONUTS WERE GONE**. So, I had to eat toast. **TOAST**. It's just **HARD BREAD!**

Then Rover yanked out the power cord before I could save my game! It's just been a really bad day and—

Bad day! Did you say "bad day"? Well, that, Jack, is something I can solve.

No, no. You don't need to solve it. I really just wanted to—

SOLVE IT! I know, I was listening.

Lucky for you, I just completed the world's first scientific cure for "the bad day"!

CUE THE ADVERTISEMENT!

Rough day at school?
I don't want to talk about it.
Worst day of your life?
YES. And possibly last!
100% A PAID TESTIMONIAL
We've got the cure!
Quint Co.'s latest! BAD-DAY-AWAY absorbs all those pesky emotions that you don't want. BAD-DAY-AWAY feels the emotions FOR YOU.*
I HAD NOT DECAPITATED AN EVIL BEAST IN WEEKS! I HAD SO MUCH PENT-UP AGGRESSION—AND NO HEALTHY WAY TO LET IT OUT.
BUT NOW, THANKS TO BAD-DAY-AWAY . . .
THOSE EMOTIONS ARE GONE! THANKS, BAD-DAY-AWAY.
AAAH . . .
SHOVEL
For real. Thanks.
BAD-DAY-AWAY! IT'S THE PUTTY THAT STOPS YOU FEELING CRUDDY!
*WARNING: May cause drowsiness, alertness, loss of appetite, increased appetite. In rare cases, head explosion may occur.

Try some!
Hey! Ow! What are you—
SMEKT!
Shh. Shh.
You'll feel better in a moment, friend.
Whoa....
That stuff works! Quint, you are the COOLEST and the BRAVEST and I hereby gift to you my entire collection of Happy Meal toys.
Another satisfied Quint Co. customer.
Now, one word of caution: the putty must be used in moderation. If not, the consequences could be . . .
Hoo, ooh! It tickles between the toes!
JACK!
I got some behind my eyeball. Is that bad?
That's too much! You'll trigger molecular evolu—
MORPH

MORPH!

Ooh, it looks like a giant Sour Patch Kid!
Please don't eat it, Jack.

Up high, putty buddy!
Fascinating. . . . Less aggressive than I had expected.

Whoa! He knows "up high, down low, too slow!"
What a cool guy.
It appears the putty creature has inherited your terrible sense of humour.

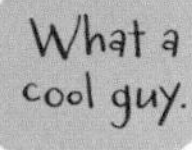
MISS!

He's into friendly wrestling time!
MERMM.
OFF THE ROPES!
RARRM!
CHAIRED!
Ow! You're supposed to fake it!
This is not friendly!
Take it easy, bud!
Watch out! My lab!
PUNCH!
KICK
It's acting as frustrated as I felt!
VIOLENCE!
BREAKING STUFF!
Of course! It's venting its frustration by destroying things!
But there may be a way to stop it. . . .

***QUINT NOTE:** Technically, the patent is still pending. But only because the patent office is currently overrun by very inventive zombies!

HELLO, QUINT. I AM YOUR INVENTION. I HAVE NO MOUTH, BUT I *MUST* DESTROY!
Hey, I think Dirk's home.
No, Jack! It's my lab . . . It has been infected by the putty! IT'S ALIVE!
LATE NIGHT HOT POCKENATOR
80's TIME MACHINE
HULK

For the record, Quint, this is doing nothing for my bad day . . .
If you had only followed my instructions, Jack!
BLAST! BALL
MOUNTAIN DEW BREWER
BREAKFAST CLUB
The Relax-a-Tron! It wants to eat us!
What are we gonna do, Quint?
No need to panic, Jack!
These are MY inventions, after all. How bad could it be . . . ?

Your contraptions and inventions. They're, like, going viral!
AND NOT IN A FUNNY MEME WAY!
They're sentient. And they're joining with the tree house. They are becoming one.
The tree house! It's tilting!
Well, that can't be good!
Aaaa aggh!
Not to worry!
I've got just the thing we need . . .
CUE ADVERTISEMENT!

The Mobile-Pong Ping-Pong Ramp-Pong!

What's happening?
The tree house is transforming. It's turning into . . .
A rocket ship?
What? No, Jack.
It's a monster . . .
I WILL DESTROY MY CREATOR!
Yipe!
AND NOW . . . INTERMISSION!

YOUR LIVES HANG BY A STRING . . .
ATTACK OF THE KILLER YO-YOS
PART THE SECOND!
TRIP!
ACTION!
SPLAT
LAFFS!
ROMANCE!
THE HORROR YOU THOUGHT YOU THREW AWAY JUST . . . COMES RIGHT BACK!

Attack of the Killer Yo-Yos Part the Second! Starring **Quint Baker**, **June Del Toro**, and **Dirk Savage**. Introducing **Jack Sullivan** as Kid Tiddlywinks. Music by June's Dad's Music Collection. Director of Photography by Whoever Was Available to Hold the Camera. Catering by Dirk Savage. Edited by June Del Toro. More Editing by June Del Toro. Too Much Editing by June Del Toro. Written by Quint Baker and Jack Sullivan. Story by Quint Baker (with a Tiny Bit of Help from Jack Sullivan). Based on a Napkin Sketch by Quint Baker and Jack Sullivan. Inspired by a Yo-Yo Quint Received from His Nana. Produced by Quint Baker and Jack Sullivan. Directed by Quint Baker and Jack Sullivan But Mostly Quint Baker.

COMING SOON TO A LIVING ROOM NEAR YOU!

Impossible odds? No one to turn to for help?
You know what time it is, Jack?
I sure do . . .
DASH!
Jack . . .
No, Jack. Heroes never run!
What about the Flash? That's, like, all he does.
It's time for a SUPERHERO UPGRADE!
I am . . . DOC BAKER: SUPER SCIENTIST AND INVENTORIST EXTRAORDINAIRE!
BRAIN FULL OF BRILLIANCE! BACKPACK FULL OF GADGETS!
HAN SHOT FIRST
And Jack is . . . SIDEKICK BOY!
GIFTED WITH REGULAR-POWERED SIDE KICKS!
KICK! KICK!

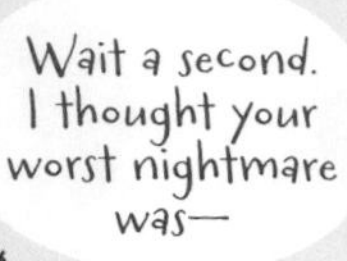

Unbelievable. ALL of my inventions, turning on their creator: ME! It's like I'm being confronted by my worst nightmare!
Wait a second. I thought your worst nightmare was—

UPLOADING... UPLOADING... UPLOADING...
Sitting down for video game time only to discover you have to install a 549-GB, 19-hour update! Or . . .

Accidentally making a peanut butter and jellyFISH sammich! Or . . .

Putting your socks on AFTER your shoes. Again.
SCHOOL
CYA

I assure you, Sidekick Boy, a sentient tree house full of come-to-life inventions turning against me, their inventor, is indeed my worst nightmare!
Although the peanut butter and jellyfish sandwich does haunt me to my very core.
I NEVER CHOSE THIS LIFE! YOU CREATED ME. SO NOW YOU MUST BE DESTROYED!
SHAKT!
Oh no! It's absorbing Big Mama! It's got a Big Mama hammer hand!
Pretty rad upgrade tho.
DESTROY! DESTROY!
FIRST . . . I WILL DESTROY YOU, QUINT BAKER, MY MAKER! THEN I WILL SAY OTHER RHYMING THINGS!
AND AFTER THAT, I WILL DESTROY WAKEFIELD. AND PRETTY SOON . . . THE WORLD!
Fisticuffles!
Fear not, Sidekick Boy. We've faced far worse than this before . . .

WORSE THINGS WE'VE FACED BEFORE!

I'LL circle! You assault!
I'd like to swap vehicles, please.
Side kick!
Side kick!
Side kick!
KICK!
KICK!
KICK!
RAAHH!!
Whoa! Big Mama hand!
SCOOCH!
C'mon, Sidekick Boy!
It's like trying to fight ALL of your inventions at once.
SCOOP!
You're right, Sidekick Lad!
Sidekick BOY.
TURN!
WAFFLER
. . . Which is bad enough!

Your mind created these inventions! Only you can stop them! We need a light bulb moment, Doc!
So how do we defeat perfection?
FLICK
AHHH!
I never said they were perfect. This is kind of all your—
You're right, Sidekick Boy.
C'mon, genius mind, gimme an idea . . .
MY FRUSTRATION IS ALL-CONSUMING. AND I WILL TAKE IT OUT ON YOU!
This bad day went from bad to worse, and then worser than ultra-WORST.
GASP! Your bad day, Jack! Of course! LIGHT BULB IDEA MOMENT!
Hey, tree house, you need a time-out!
Meet the LIGHT BULB IDEA CANNON!
FOOSH!
PUSH!
ZZZAP!
ZAP!
BUT I DON'T WANT A TIME-OUUUUUT!

I'm sorry, Jack. This is my fault. It started this morning . . .
I didn't let you share your feelings. Instead, I rushed to solve them with science. I should have simply sat and listened.
The putty then took your pent-up, bad-day frustration and lashed out. And instead of listening, we just started fighting. So, giant putty-tree-house-tech friend . . . how ARE you feeling . . . ?
WELL, NOW THAT YOU ASK . . .
Wait, so we're just gonna sit around and talk about our feelings now?
You are. Meanwhile, I'm going to dismantle the beast.
A short time later . . .
Sometimes it just feels good to talk about your feelings.
Y'KNOW WHAT? IT DOES. IT REALLY DOES.
Kick, kick, kick!

I've felt frustrated like that too!
I hear you! And can relate! Sweet high-five moves, bro.
THANKS, GUYS!
THIS IS A BETTER WAY TO EXPEND MY ENERGY!
This is the real version of Bad-Day-Away!
Later still . . .
WOW, THAT REALLY MADE A DIFFERENCE!
THANK YOU BOTH FOR LISTENING.
What? Oh, right. I mean, of course!
HAWKEYE
I WAS ONLY ACTING ON THE EMOTIONS I WAS GIVEN.
I DIDN'T MEAN ANY HARM.

Maybe there is no scientific cure for a bad day, after all.
Uh, where is this **heroic wind** coming from?

We're home! What's the orange stuff? And what's with the costumes?
Killer cosplay. Can I vent? We just had the **WORST** day.
QUINT'S LAB!

Sometimes, when you've got big emotions, you just need to **talk** about them. And you need someone to **listen**. Science is no substitute for sharing how we feel with the people who care most:

Our friends.
TELL ME ALL YOUR PROBLEMS!
Oh no! Not again!
To be continued ... (Eventually ...)

IN THE NEXT EXCITING ADVENTURE OF

DOC BAKER:
I battle the **GADGET GOBLIN FROM BEYOND!** And my loud sidekick, Sidekick Boy, tags along.
I do little side kicks! Kick, kick, kick.
END!

Ooh, good stuff, Quint! Action! Humour! That had it aLL. You should win some awards or something. Definitely a starred Kirkus review.
And your drawings are on fire, dude! Almost as good as, like, a professional comic iLLustrator!
Hold up. Sidekick Boy? You made me SIDEKICK BOY?!?
I think I have a crush on that super-smart Doc Baker guy. Blush!
Doc Baker was Quint.
Oh, I know . . .

This comic made me look silly. And I **never** look silly!
SLAM!
I resent this sound effect!
SLAPPED SILLY!
A MONSTROUS HAND HAS BREACHED THE SHRUB FORTRESS!
Get down!
YOU ARE FINISHED!

KRAK!
Quick, Sidekick Boy! Barricade the door!
Quint, if that catches on—I'm gonna write a revenge comic! Where you play second fiddle to me!
You wouldn't dare infringe upon my other series, First Fiddle Quint and the Trumpet Kid!
ONE MOMENT! FORGET THE INVADING TENTACLES! QUINT! I WAS HARDLY EVEN A CAMEO IN YOUR STORY!
I SHOULD HAVE CHOPPED THIS CARTOON TOME IN HALF WHEN I HAD THE CHANCE.
SUCH NONSENSE!
NO! DONT!
You totally should! Good idea!
SUPER INVENTORIST DUDE!

No, Skaelka. Everyone's got a right to their own story. You'LL get your turn.
But first— it's time for mine . . .
This is the tale of a run-in I had with some Rifters.
Lousy interdimensional pirates . . . Love to hate 'em.
Oh yeah. Those guys are The Worst.
And it begins once upon a time at Warg's . . .

DIRK SAVAGE IN...
THE GOOD, THE BAD, AND THE SAVAGE
story by Max Brallier
art by Christopher Mitten
colour by Brennan Wagner
Hello, pumpkin. How are you this fine mornin'?
OJ

Trot careful, Herman.
Look at these pumpkins the wrong way and...
BOOM! Blow you right up.
Huh?!
Oof!
Somethin's up.
Oh no. . . . Warg! I'm comin'!
MOAN . . .

What happened?
How come all your eyeballs came racin' back home like that?
A CREATURE . . .
IN A CAPE. . . .
ONE EYEBALL WAS STOLEN. . . .
Wait, sorry, but don't you have, like . . . tons of eyeballs?
Like, infinity?
NOT INFINITY. NOT EVEN CLOSE.
I WAS BORN WITH A SET NUMBER OF EYEBALLS. ONCE THEY ARE ALL GONE, THEN MY LIFE IS COMPLETE. I WILL PERISH. SO EACH ONE IS VALUABLE. . . .
But, Warg, you gave me one of your eyeballs that time I was almost zombified.
It saved my life—but it was also destroyed. I returned it—but by then it was a just a floppy dead thing.
YES. I FORFEITED ONE TO HELP YOU. BECAUSE IT WAS THE RIGHT THING TO DO.

I won't return without that eyeball, Warg.
That's a promise.
That li'l thief thinks they got away clean, huh. Well, ol' Dirk's about to dirty things up a bit....
Hee-ya, Herman!

Later . . .
Tail prints. We're on the track, Herman.
This pace, I reckon we'LL be on them by dusk.
KA-KLINK-KLINK!
SURPRISE LASSO!
AIIEE!
SNAG!
FLIT!

Why, you ain't nothin' but a kid.
I'm sorry! I didn't mean to steal, I'm not a thief usually. But, y'see, our elder, Wyther—she was wounded by Rifters.
Rifters?
That's right. Meeks's been attacking our home every night, trying to drive us out.
Wyther's not long to live
This eyeball is the only hope she's got. . . . She only needs to nuzzle it, see, so you can have it back after—
Lemme think. . . .
Seventeen minutes later . . .
You still thinkin', or . . . ?
Still thinkin'.
Another seventeen minutes later . . .
Well, all right. I'll help, little one. But we need to be jack-rabbit quick. C'mon.

So, why're these Rifters attackin' you, anyway?
On account of us having the only working Sugar-Slurp machine in these parts. They're trying to steal it, and that ain't right.
Meeks—he's the Rifters' leader. He craves that sweet, sugary nectar. His whole band of Rifters are big-time sugar heads. But that Sugar-Slurp machine is ours! We found it and fixed it up real good!
Wyther has a plan for the Sugar-Slurp.
Our whole band will start makin' our way west, stopping at outposts, settlements, and the like. Make an honest living selling the frozen goodness.
Grumble...
What's 'a matter?
You don't like frozen sugar drinks?
Nah, not that.
I don't like being lost. And that, right now, is what we are.

Zzzz . . .
I got a feelin' this here hut could be the answer to our prayers. . . .

How ya doin'?
We were headin' for the Dairy Barn in Stahlstown, but got a bit turned around.
Yeah, we're lost.
HELLO! WELCOME! GREETINGS! GOOD TO SEE YA!
Huh. Kinda expected you to tell us to scram.
YOU KIDDING? YOU KNOW HOW BORING IT IS HERE ALL ALONE? I'VE BEEN PLAYING TWISTER BY MYSELF—YOU HAVE ANY IDEA HOW SAD THAT IS?
COME IN! PLEASE!

Some time later…
We're trying to find our way back to this little one's home.
It's the Dairy Barn off the main road.
There are Rifters nearby, if that helps.
I CAN SHOW YOU THE WAY, YES. . . . BUT NOT FOR FREE. . . .
I was afraid of this.
Conjurer gibberish. Lots of cryptic prattle that we don't have time for.
OK, YOU WANT ME TO CUT RIGHT TO IT? I WILL OFFER YOU A CHALLENGE. IF YOU DEFEAT ME, I'LL TELL YOU HOW TO GET WHERE YOU WANNA BE GETTIN'. HOWEVER, IF YOU LOSE . . .
YOU MUST WEAR THIS T-SHIRT FOR THE REST OF YOUR DAYS.
AND ALSO, YOU'LL RECEIVE NO INFORMATION.
I REQUESTED A FAVOR FROM YURSL THE UNKNOWING AND ALL I GOT WAS THIS LOUSY T-SHIRT
All right, then. What's the challenge?

FROM BEYOND THE ARC, EYES CLOSED.
Wait.... HORSE? Really?
I thought I was gonna have to drink weird stew from a cauldron or something.
YURST
That's HORSE!
THAT DID NOT GO AS I HAD EXPECTED.
Winners chill, losers spill. So start spillin'—show us how we get to the kid's home.

FOLLOW THE PATH YOU SEE ON THE IDIOT BOX. WHEN THE ROAD FORKS, STAY LEFT.
Much obliged.
Yes, thanks— now c'mon, c'mon, we gotta go! Got to get home before sunset— the Rifters always attack in the evening!

DAIRY BARN
Here we are. Home sweet home. The Rifters don't usually attack until nightfall.
Well, let's giddyup then. Daylight's burnin'.
HAVE YOU BROUGHT THE EYE, EEWEE? THE SOONER I CAN GET BACK TO HEALTH, THE SOONER WE CAN END THIS....
Yes, great one. I have retrieved it.
AND WHO'S THIS?

This is Mr. Savage. He helped me and—
We need to return that eyeball lickety-split. So let's get a move on, huh?
I MUST CRADLE THE EYEBALL THROUGH THE NIGHT. IT RADIATES ENOUGH ENERGY TO BRING ME BACK TO HEALTH. THEN I CAN END THIS TORMENT.
Then I'll be outside. Waitin' for what's to come. . . .
Later . . .
It's been dark for a while. Maybe they won't come tonight.
Doubt it. That's the problem with bad folks. They say they're gonna do somethin', they usually do.

WELL, LOOK AT THIS ONE HERE—FIT FOR FRYIN'. STANDING GUARD, HALF-PINT?
SO, THE LITTLE ONE WENT TO YOU FOR HELP, HUH?
HOW ABOUT WE GET TO KNOW EACH OTHER?
Not exactly. But that's how things are now.
How about you turn around, leave these folks alone.
NAH. I GOT MY OWN FOLKS TO LOOK AFTER.
THUNK!
You stay back, little one!
Don't think so!

WHACK!
PLING!
Slap shot!
No sugar for you!
HUFF AND PUFF ALL YOU WANT—WE'RE NOT LEAVING WITHOUT THAT EYEBALL.
Huh? Thought you wanted—
THE SUGAR-SLURP? HA! NAH. SEE, WE HURT THE OLD ONE KNOWING SHE'D SEEK THE EYEBALL.
IT'S THE EYEBALL WE WANT—ALWAYS HAS BEEN. THOSE EYEBALLS HAVE POWERS.
What's he yammerin' about??
I've no idea, Mr. Savage! Honest!
KA-KA-KRAKKK!

What on—
Hot spit!
She went from "dying elderly lady monster" to "super-scary monster" real quick.
KRACK!
KRUNCH!
THIS ENDS TODAY, FOUL RIFTERS!
AIEEE!
FLING!

No! Not the little one! Don't hurt—
Oof!
SLAM!
SQOOF!
Hmm...

STAY BACK, OR ELSE!
So, this is what you want? The eyeball? Then here. Take it.
WHAT'RE YOU PLAYIN' AT?
You leave them alone. For good. That's it. You take the eyeball and ride. Far and fast and don't ever look back—or else. . . .
DEAL.
Catch.

PLEASURE DOING BUSINESS WITH YOU.

LET'S RIDE!

Later . . .
But what if they come back?
They won't. That's a promise.
WE ARE MUCH OBLIGED, MR. SAVAGE. SOMEDAY, I HOPE WE CAN REPAY YOU FOR YOUR AID.

I'LL see you around, little one.
Remember—careful where you point that thing.

Goodbye, Mr. Savage! Goodbye!

Much later . . .
Warg, I'm sorry. I'm so sorry . . .
. . . that it took so long. But . . .
Here's your eyeball. Returned. As promised.
YOU OWED ME NO DEBT, SAVAGE. BUT I THANK YOU.
THE ONE WHO TOOK THE EYEBALL. THE VILLAIN. WHAT HAPPENED TO THEM?
The one who took it was no villain. And the real villain— let's just say, well . . . they got what they had comin'. . . .

WITH THIS SPHERE—
WE WILL BECOME POWERFUL ENOUGH TO SEARCH THE ENTIRE LAND FOR SUGAR-SLURP! WE WILL RAID AND WE WILL DRINK!
OUR THIRST WILL BE QUENCHED, OVER AND OVER!
WHAT? BUT . . . THIS IS JUST . . .
PUMPKIN! IT'S JUST A PUMPKIN!
I WILL FIND YOU, DIRK SAVAGE!
KA-BOOM!
SEED SHRAPNEL!
END!

Hold up— You and Warg hang out . . .
without ME?
Hang on. You met like a real, live witch? I hope we bump into her again someday . . .
Wait—Warg's pumpkins blow up??? No wonder my tummy's been acting weird.
ENOUGH! I GROW BORED OF THESE TALES!
SLAM!
It proves I'm awesome. I think I proved that. Yup. I did.
NONE OF THESE STORIES PROVE ANYBODY WORTHY OF ANYTHING!
Relax, Skaelka. I'm pretty sure I know the story you want to tell. And it's not just yours, Skaelka— it's OURS . . .
YES! TELL IT, YOUNG JUNE! PROVE OUR SUPERIORITY TO THESE BLABBERMOUTHS AND THEIR ECCENTRIC, NON-AXE-CENTRIC STORIES!

Get on with it! We already know I'm winning this . . .
Yeah, I could use a nap.
Commence at your pleasure, June!
Am I in your story? Be a lot cooler if I was . . .
TELL OUR STORY WELL, JUNE. WITH NO EMBELLISHMENT! BUT DO NOT HOLD BACK MY HEROICS! OR ROVER'S INVOLVEMENT! OR CLAUDIA!
DO NOT FORGET CLAUDIA!
Duh. I'll tell the whole story, Skaelka . . .
AND PUT MUCH FOCUS ON THE OUTRAGEOUS ODDS! IT WAS A REAL SCRAP! A BRILLIANT BRAWL!
Oh, it was a slugfest, all right . . .

JUNE & SKAELKA IN
KETTLE TO THE MEDAL
JOE'S PIZZA
GO!
Thanks for the trophies, Parker Middle School.
Perfect for Fling-N-Fetch!
FLING-N-FETCH . . . AND DESTROY!
Go deep, Skaelka! Like, really deep!
story by
Max Brallier
art by
Lorena Alvarez Gómez
JUNE, YOU ARE A FOOL!
YOU CANNOT FIRE IT THIS FAR!
Oh yeah? Watch me!
FLING!
Whoops. Too deep.

SWISH!
My bad!
YES. TOO FAR.
TRY AGAIN, HUMAN JUNE.
ARF?
FASTER, FOUR LEGS! WE WILL BLAST IT FROM THE SKY!
GRUNT
THROW!
FLY, CLAUDIA! FLY FAST AND STRIKE FATAL!
MISS!
FAIL!
OH DARN.
FLARFGH!
KER-KRASH!

Rover! You OK?
DO YOU SEE HER? WHERE IS MY CLAUDIA?!
Oh... Oh wow.
<Sniff!>
That smell.
WHAT... WHAT... IS THIS PLACE, JUNE?
ICE Cream
THIS LOOKS TO BE THE LARGEST CELEBRATION OF A HUMAN CHILD'S DELIVERY DAY I HAVE EVER SET EYES UPON.
Huh, what? No, Skaelka—it's a carnival.
Wakefield's official summer kickoff. My parents took me every year.
Everything must've just **stopped**. Right when, y'know, everything else **started**.
WHAT IS THAT TREMENDOUS SCENT?
<INHALE!>
Kettle corn.
And it's not a tremendous scent.
It's the **worst odour ever.**

COME. I NEED TO RECOVER MY AXE.
Hold on, hold on.
Let's blow this place. Don't like it. Don't wanna be here.
It's just an axe, right?
INCORRECT!
CLAUDIA IS NOT JUST ANY AXE. WE HAVE BEEN THROUGH MANY ADVENTURES AND DONE MUCH SLAYING TOGETHER.
YOU KNOW MY MOTTO: NO AXE LEFT BEHIND.
That's your motto?
IT IS NOW.
It's just . . . I don't have great memories of this place.
THEN YOU WAIT HERE, COWERING IN FEAR OF INANIMATE RECOLLECTIONS. I WILL RETRIEVE CLAUDIA.
Fine, ya stubborn brute! But as soon as we find Claudia, we split.
RUFFMPH.
YES, YES. NOW SHOW ME THIS WORLD OF CARNIVAL!

GOOD TIMES AT THE CARNIVAL

ANOTHER NECKLACE FOR JUNE!
ANOTHER NECKLACE FOR JUNE!
HOUSE

Love METER
SKAELKA IS NO "DEAD FISH"!

FASTER, COLOURFUL STEED!
FASTER!

QUICKLY! TO THE BIG SPINNING CIRCLE!
NOPE. I am **not** getting on the Gravity-Spinster
EVER.

Hey— YIKES! Clown Zombie.

GLURGH.

WHAT KIND OF WEIRD HUMAN-CARNIVAL THING IS THIS?
IT IS FUN TO SIT ABOVE A BOX OF LIQUID?
No, no. The fun is for **us.** Not the one sitting.

Watch . . .
FLING!
TING!

MER?
KER-SPLASH!

AHH, THE OL' PLUNGE-THE-TRAITOR-INTO-THE-ACID-VAT GAME!
WE HAVE THAT IN MY DIMENSION, THOUGH IT IS MUCH MORE FUN. THEIR TRAITOROUS SCREAMS REALLY TICKLE THE FUNNY BONES.

Wait. Something's **weird** about this guy, though.
HUMAN JUNE . . .
WHAT IS IT?
Something I . . . can't quite . . .
GRB-GRB-GRB . . .
Whoa. Wouldja look at that!
BLEGKT! BLEG!
BLEGKT!

Do you see that thing inside its mouth! It's like a little monster SLUG!
GRODY!
RAWRRR! RRROWL!
RAWRR!
GNNNNNGHH . . .
CRASH!
OH YES, NOW THE CARNIVAL FUN BEGINS!
Nope! Fun's over . . . and now's the time to RUN!
GAH!

They're everywhere!
I KNOW! IF I HAD CLAUDIA, THIS WOULD TRULY BE A DAY TO REMEMBER!
Oof.
Skaelka! I think I tripped over—
TRIP!
CREAK...
CLAUDIA!
REUNITED!

HAUNTED MINE
Wait, no! Stop the ride!
CLAUDIA AND SKAELKA ARE COMING!
ROLL!

SCOOCH OVER. THIS SEAT IS TOO SMALL FOR MY MUSCLES.
Ow, hey. Your spikes are pokin' me.
RAWLF!
HA-HA! THOSE BEASTS ARE BOGUS!
BUT THESE ONES ARE REAL! MUCH MORE SATISFYING!
Skaelka, no! We don't destroy zombies!
Those zombies were once in someone's family. We have to be careful.
WHAT'S THAT, CLAUDIA? JUNE RUINS ALL THE FUN? YES, YES, I AGREE.
Skaelka, I know the axe doesn't talk.
Something's up with these zombies. They're **different**.
And we need to find out **why**.
We gotta get a closer look at those slug things. They're making these zombies act **extra dangerous**.

RAAWWGGHHR!
YOU NEED YELLOW-TONGUED ZOMBIE . . . ?
CLAUDIA WILL GET YOU YELLOW-TONGUED ZOMBIE!
CLANG!
RAWWWGGHR!
Whoa, Claudia!
WHAMPH!
The slug … looks … like it's **controlling** the zombie … like a little pilot.

Skaelka, grab it!
I THOUGHT YOU WOULD NEVER ASK!
Uh-oh. We have company. . . .
Wow. These little things are **quite** acrobatic.
SKKSSSHHH!
SLIME-LEAP!
That is so not sanitary!
ICK!
MMMPPGHHPH!
Oh, no way . . .
THE SLUGS CAN . . . JUMP HOSTS!
TeLL Claudia we're getting off this ride!

MIRRORS
Faster! In there!
FUN HOUSE
I WILL SMASH EACH AND EVERY ONE OF YOU ODDLY SIMILAR-YET-DISTORTED-LOOKING SLUG ZOMBIES!
Ooh, that's a couple thousand years of bad luck, easy. . . .
OK, these things are freaking me out. You ever seen anything like them before?
No. AND THEY BETTER NOT TRY TO CONTROL SKAELKA.
SHATTER-SMASH!
Meep!
BLASTY-BLAST!
SKAELKA WILL NOT ADMIT FEAR. HOWEVER, WE SHOULD NOT LINGER. JUNE, YOU PREVIOUSLY WANTED SKAELKA TO "GO DEEP!"
I AGREE.
WE SHOULD GO REAL DEEP, DEEPLY OUT OF THIS—WHAT DO YOU HUMANS CALL IT?—TRASH FIRE.

Hold up, wait a minute, stop! **What are we doing?**
WE ARE GOING REAL DEEP AND GOING HOME!
DID YOU NOT HEAR ME? CLAUDIA HEARD ME!
We can't leave now.
If we don't stop them, who will? These zombies are **different**—fast and extra scary! Just imagine if they got loose back in town. . . .
HMMM . . .
Hey! What did I do?! Why am I in this weird zombie daydream fantasy!?
YES, YOU ARE RIGHT. IT WOULD BE BAD. BUT QUITE ENJOYABLE TO SEE!
C'mon. Let's shut these dudes down.

Wait, do you hear that? It sounds like they are talking.
I CANNOT HEAR THEM WELL ENOUGH. IF THEY WERE CLOSER, MAYBE. . . .
BIGGEST PRIZES AROUND
Skaelka, can you translate?
I've got an idea. . . .
KEET . . .
KEEEKT, KEET.
SKOOOT-SLEET.
3
Well? What's the deal?
THIS IS HUMILIATING. THAT IS THE DEAL.
I mean what are they saying!!
IT IS AN . . . OLD LANGUAGE. THEY SPEAK OF BLOOD AND WAR AND . . .
AND EATING EVERY LAST HUMAN IN THIS DIMENSION.
Anything else?
YES. THEY SMELL YOU.
Crud.

KEEEET! SLEET! SLOOT! KEEET!
KETTLE CORN
KER-CRASH! KRUNCH!
RAAAGGHH!! ROWR!!!
Rover to the rescue! Head for Salty Joe's Kettle Corn Emporium! I might have another idea. . . .
MOMENTS LATER . . .
WHY ARE WE EATING INSTEAD OF FIGHTING? EATING IS WHAT IS DONE AFTER THE BATTLING IS COMPLETE. . . .
KETTLE CORN
We're not eating. We're getting ready to fight.
You see, kettle corn has lots of salt—and slugs hate salt. At least, normal Earth ones do.
BUT WHAT . . . WHAT IS THIS "KETTLE CORN," JUNE?
The whole reason I didn't want to come in here in the first place. . . .
SHARE WITH ME, JUNE— JUST AS I HAVE SHARED MANY OF MY STORIES OF COMBAT WITH YOU.

The last time I was here, I was eight years old. And I overdid it. Big-time. Fried EVERYTHING. Fried dough, fried Oreos, fried pickles on a stick, fried pickles not on a stick. And I topped it all off with five bags of the freshest, saltiest kettle corn that ever existed. . . .

I felt sick, but I got on the Gravity-Spinster anyway. . . .

I refused to miss out. . . .

And halfway through the ride, I—

EJECTED THE PARTIALLY DIGESTED FOOD-STUFF UPWARD THROUGH YOUR MOUTH HOLE.

Oh! No! My clothes!

Someone stop the ride!

It's in my hair!

It's in my ear!

It's in my ear hair!

JUNE, THAT STORY WAS TRULY REVOLTING. AND GLORIOUS.

THANK YOU FOR SHARING.

I'm happy it made you happy.

But it was just about the most embarrassing thing that—

SSSSHHHHHSSSS!
Aggh!
KEKEEEKT!
KEEET-HIIISSSSS!!!

Skaelka, you go fire up the Gravity-Spinster. I'm gonna lead 'em there.

POP! POP! POP!
TAK TAK TAK!
This is a terrible idea. . . .
GREAT! CLAUDIA AND SKAELKA LOVE TERRIBLE IDEAS!
TAK!
PAMF!
Kettle corn! Get your kettle corn here!
Step right up and OPEN WIDE!
TAK TAK TAK!
PAMF!
YES! Salt does work on these zombie-controlling slugs!
Keep it coming, gang. Don't quit. You know you wanna eat me.
RARRGHHR!
HISSSS!

BAM!
PAMF!
PAFT!
Can't believe I'm going on this ride again. . . .
READY WHEN YOU ARE!
Rover, get the door! Skaelka, hit it!
HISSS!!!
BAM!
KA-CHUNK!
VRROOOOM!
HURRAGGHH!
KEEKT! KEEKT!
KEEEEEE—
KEEEEEE!
SLAM SLAM SLAM SLAM

A SHORT TIME LATER . . .
MOAAAAAN!
Well, at least this time I wasn't the one that made the mess. Still pretty gross, though . . .
THERE IS ONE LEFT! AND IT'S MAKING A SHAMBLE FOR IT!
YOU WILL NOT BE ABLE TO FIRE A TROPHY THAT FAR!
I'm not firing a trophy. I'm firing Claudia. . . .
GO DEEP!
HEE-YA!
FIRE!
LOOK AT THAT ACCURACY!
JUNE SHOULD BE QUARTERBACK FOR THE CLEVELAND BROWNS. OR THE CINCINNATI BENGALS. ANY OHIO TEAM, REALLY!

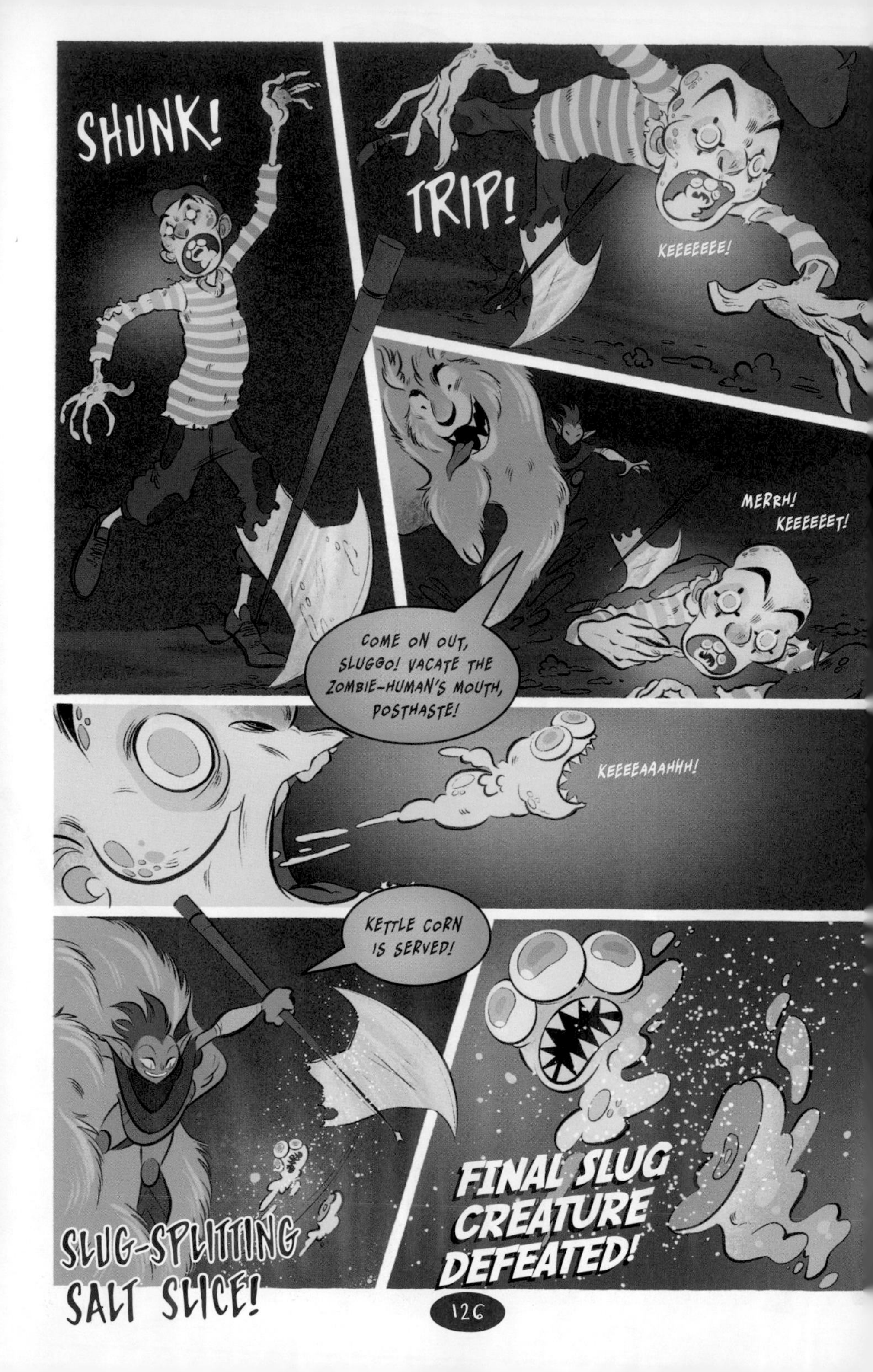
SHUNK!
TRIP!
KEEEEEEE!
MERRH!
KEEEEEET!
COME ON OUT, SLUGGO! VACATE THE ZOMBIE-HUMAN'S MOUTH, POSTHASTE!
KEEEEAAAHHH!
KETTLE CORN IS SERVED!
SLUG-SPLITTING SALT SLICE!
FINAL SLUG CREATURE DEFEATED!

I guess this is why we have rules.
Like, why we don't hurt the zombies, because they used to be people.
And sometimes, even the zombies need our help. If we don't stay true to ourselves and those values . . .
then we're just as bad as the enemies we're facing. Maybe worse.
STUPID HUMAN MORAL CODE.
Oh, hush. Time to go home.
That evening at Skaelka's pad . . .
WELL, CLAUDIA, YOU'RE BACK HOME.
WITH ALL YOUR FRIENDS.
You have GOT to be kidding!
WOMP WOMP.
END!

Oh, I get it. Slug fest. Because of the slugs.
Thanks, Jack. It's always funnier when you have to explain it.
Wait, Skaelka— how many axes do you actually have?
Well, that wraps up the stories! Which means . . .
IT'S GO TIME. If someone still wants to take on that monster single-handedly—we gotta vote on it.
Everyone, write down your vote. One vote per storyteller. Then put it in this conveniently placed hat.
Hold on, is that a regulation-size conveniently placed hat?
It appears to be. However, it could—
SMASH!

BANG!
BANG!
BANG!

Seven minutes and plenty of tentacle bashing later . . .
OK, and . . . that's one vote for Jack, one vote for Quint, one vote for Dirk, one vote for Globlet, and one vote for June and Skaelka.
I didn't think it needed to be said, but . . . you're not allowed to vote for your own story!
I didn't. I voted for Quint. I like Sidekick Boy. That character's gonna be a breakout hit.
Aww, Dirk. I voted for you, too!
BUDDIES!
I . . . voted for mine.
Me too.
I VOTED FOR US, JUNE. IT WAS MY DUTY. OUR STORY WAS SUPERIOR!

SO, WHAT NOW? MY AXE THIRSTS FOR MONSTER TENTACLE!
Well, in the event of a tie—I guess we all do this thing . . .
EVERYONE TOGETHER!

We look GOOD.

WAIT! PLEASE, DON'T!
Cancel the attack!
Abort! Abort!
Can't cancel a fight midair! Not how it works!

CRASH!
This is awkward.
Are we in trouble now? We're gonna get eaten.
I CALL DO-OVERS.
Aw, man, my gadget got banged up!
CHILL, GUYS, I JUST WANTED TO HANG! I SMELLED YOUR TREATS AND HEARD YOUR TUNES AND WANTED TO JOIN IN THE FUN!
WHADDAYA SAY . . . PALS?
Um . . .
Sure, friend! The more the merrier!
We're trading stories—got any good ones?
OOH, DO I EVER!

Eight minutes later . . .
. . . AND THEN I ERUPTED FROM THE THING'S CHEST AND ATE ITS HEAD! IT WAS REALLY, REALLY GROSS. BUT NOT AS GROSS AS THE TIME I–
Classic!
NOW THAT'S WHAT I'M TALKING ABOUT! CLAUDIA IS PLEASED!
Ooh, I'm gonna use this story for my next comic!
Best story of the day, no doubt.
Whatever. My story was better . . . It had ME in it.
END! YAY! BOOK OVER!

RECORD SCRATCH!

Hold the landline! It's time for our story!

EVIE SNARK & GHAZT THE GENERAL IN . . .

THE EPIC TALE OF EPIC STUFF YOU NEVER SAW HAPPEN (BUT SHOULD PROBABLY KNOW ABOUT!)

THIS TALE WILL EXPLAIN PERTINENT EVENTS BETWEEN BOOKS FOUR AND SEVEN.

story by
Max Brallier

art by Douglas Holgate

TIME FOR A QUICK RECAP, POPPETS!
Hi. I'm Evie Snark, evil mastermind.
The big one-armed dude here is Meathook.
RRR-RR-RTT!
Whatcha got there, Evie?
This? Sigh. Guess I need to narrate this thing.
I was lolally just minding my own evil business trying to summon interdimensional giant monsters to rule the Earth. And you need a powerful object to do that with, see? I got word that this kid, Jeff, had a broken bat or whatever. And I needed it.
Jack.
Huh?
His name is Jack. Sullivan.
OMG, really?
WHO CARES.
Anyway:
OK, so yeah. I took it from the kid. Whatever. Sue me.
Adults are totally allowed lo sleal from children.

And see—it worked. I chose to make the portal at my former fave hangout, the ABC Block Smasher Cinema, and it was opening up without a hitch.
Former?
Never played Snyder's *Justice League* director's cut. Dead to me. Also, the world ended.
And natch:
There was **one** small hitch.
THWACK!!
Jeff frikkin' Smithsonian.
Jack. Sulliva—
YEAH: HEARD YOU THE FIRST TIME.
What can I say? The kid—a stranger really—aimed to stop me, and succeeded. Very rude.

And so just like that—Ghazt, General of the Great Rezzőch, had been fused into a giant rat with action figure parts.
ALAS.
BURP.
Dummy got his widdle wiffleball bat back....
And Meathook was crushed and lost to us underneath the nosebleed seats... My sweet guy.
YIP!

But Ghazt's power all went to his tail. And we at least still had tha—
HAH! STRIKE TRUE, CLAUDIA!
Oh, right. We scuffled with those dang kids again and one of their monster friends hacked the tail off. LOL!
Aaaaaaand now we are both circling the drain, metaphorically and literally.
Anywho. That about sums it up for ya.
I suppose there's a lesson in there somewhere, but I'm a villain.
We don't do lessons.
Eh. Just read:
Exciting segue backstory! Go!

MY TAIL! WHERE IS IT?? DO YOU HAVE IT?! TELL ME YOU HAVE IT!
Do I look like I have it??
GLOOSH!
GET OFF MY HEAD! I HATE THIS!
GLUB
Oh, relax. Rats live in sewers. You should feel right at home!
Uh-oh. We're about to do a Peter Pan!
I WILL CRADLE YOU. BUT NOT OUT OF AFFECTION.
FREEZE FRAME!
It was at this very moment that I first began to truly, truly regret bringing Ghazt to this dimension.
AHHHHHHHHH! EEEEEEeeeeeekk!
SPLASH!

Hours later . . .
Just wait . . . Someday . . .
This will all make for a terrifically tragic backstory . . .
The nobody who . . .
Erm?
DORITO BACKSTROKE . . . CHEEZ-IT WAVE POOL. YES . . . BRING ME MORE . . .
What happened?
EWWW! NO! No toes. Don't like any feet. Especially not rat feet!
MERMAID'S COVE
NO VACANCY
AHHH!
AHHH!

BE GONE, FLYING NUISANCES!
HA!
TAIL NUB SWIPE FAIL!
MY TAIL! MY ABILITY TO CONTROL THE UNDEAD! GONE!
I CAN'T BELIEVE YOU SUMMONED ME TO THIS AWFUL REALM! I CAN'T BELIEVE I ANSWERED!
Don't blame my dimension! You never would have lost your tail if you weren't a big lazy bum!
I summoned you 'cause the book said you were a great servant of Rezzoch. Instead, I got the world's most absurd couch potato!
I AM NO POTATO CHAIR! I AM GHAZT, THE GENERAL, A COSMIC TERROR! I AM—
AIEEE! MY SPLINTERED NUB HOWLS IN AGONY! MY WOUND MUST BE HEALED!
WAGGLE
WAIT! DO YOU SMELL THAT??!? IT IS . . . EVIL. EVIL MOST FOUL!
SNIFF
SNIFF
SNIFF

I don't smell anything. But rats smell good. I mean—they're good at smelling.
YES! THIS BODY'S NOSTRIL FEATURE IS POWERFUL! AND IT DETECTS EVIL. EVIL THAT IS . . . A COSMIC SERVANT, LOYAL TO BEŽŽOCH! IN THIS DIMENSION!
SNIFF
SNIFF
THE CREATURE IS NOT SO FAR FROM HERE. AND—YES—IT IS UNDERGROUND. THESE VINES MAY LEAD TO IT. . . .
SNIFF
MY POWER MAKES ME THE MOST FEARED CREATURE IN ANY DIMENSION!
I NEED IT BACK! DO YOU UNDERSTAND?
Sure. It's like if Thor was evil, became a rat, and then someone snagged Mjolnir.
A COSMIC SERVANT IS LOYAL TO BEŽŽOCH—AND BY EXTENSION, LOYAL TO ME. FIND THE CREATURE SO IT MAY HELP RETRIEVE MY TAIL. THEN I SHALL COMMAND AN ARMY. AND YOU . . .
YOU WILL SIT BESIDE ME.
PAT PAT
<Sigh.>
Fine.
I didn't trust it. I didn't trust much of anything. But I had no other choice—I had hitched my carriage to Ghazt.

So, I set out in search of this mysterious Cosmic Servant . . . .
I felt like a video game character. The hero in an RPG. But not in a good way. I was doing errands for the ultimate rat-faced NPC.
Any Servants of Ŗeżżőcħ down here?
THE UNDER GROUND RECORDS
USED NEW
Ehh, probably not what he meant.
OH HIIIIIII.

And then I struck pay dirt.
BOOM
BANG

BOOM!
BOOM!
BANG
Sorta . . .

WHOA!
BAM!
SKREEEEE!
SLICE!

SKEE-ARRR!
Come on! I dare ya!

HISSSS
MISS!
SWIPE

Eek! Shouldn't have taunted it...!

SMACK!
AHH!

FLIP

THUD
Oof!

GRRRRM.
BRRRRM.

RRRRUUMBLE!
?!
Um, do you feel that too?

VINE ERUPTION!
What the what?!
SKEE-YOWWLL!
SNAGGED!
SHIIIIKE!
YANKED! PULLED!

Um. That's new.
Ghazt said underground . . .
So, down the monster hole I went . . .
Looks like somebody's leaking.

A few weeks ago, I was finally assembling the Cabal of the Cosmic! Now I'm trekking through a gnarly monster tunnel.
Harumph . . .
I walked for hours, following the trail of ooze.
Until, finally, the scent of evil— and the scent of rotting monsters— led me to my destination . . .
Whoa. This is . . .
SO COOL!

Yikes. Feeding on monsters, huh? And you don't even bother cooking them?
Based on the super-foul stink here, I'm guessing you're the Servant of Rezzöch?
I get it—you don't like to talk while eating. I'm the same way.
I'LL just wait here until you're ready.
Hours passed.
It became clear to me that he would not be waking for some time.
So I left. I returned to Ghazt—and told him what I had found.
He was happy.
I AM HAPPY!
Ghazt told me to return—every day, until the monstrous Servant awoke. And I went. Because Ghazt promised me this was how we'd get our power back.
"We."

So, I returned to the cavern, again and again, over the weeks that followed.
Gooooood morning! Brought bagels. Little mouldy, lotsa stale—but you don't seem picky. How ya doin' today?
But after six days, I had taught myself to juggle, beaten my Tetris high score, and scrubbed a year's worth of monster guts from my sneakers. And I had had enough.
Any closer to waking up?
I'm down here, doing Ghazt's bidding—and he's up there watching cartoons!
I should be the one watching cartoons!!!
BISH
I wasn't aiming, but the ball nearly pegged that big hunk of wall-mounted interdimensional evil right in the nose.
And that's when it hit me. Surrounded by rotting monster carcasses and decaying bones . . .
KICK!
I would no longer rely on others to help me. From then on, I'd rely only on myself.

I went searching for my ball. It had landed in a monster's empty eye socket.
The ball bobbed as the wet lump convulsed.
The lump heaved as the Cosmic Servant fed—sucking the dead monster's guts like a breakfast smoothie. I watched the vines jerk and snap.
And that image—it reminded me of something . . .
I had photocopied a few of the most important pages from *Interdimensional Terrors: A History of the Cabal of the Cosmic*.*
ZIP
Where were those pages . . . Not the Conjuration of Agony. No, not Painful Resurrection. Not Suffering Locusts.
Where was—
YES! Brutish Transmutify! Exactly as I remember it.
It was suddenly clear what I had to do—as clear as Wonder Woman's jet. And if it worked, I would never be anybody's servant again . . .
*AUTHOR'S NOTE: See *The Last Kids on Earth and the Cosmic Beyond*. Jack steals the book! It's a big deal!

The next day, when I returned—I was happy. I had the makings of a plan.
♪♫♪ Evie Snark, Evie Snark, does whatever . . . ♫
And on that same happy day, at long last, the Servant awoke.
HEY! FINALLY!
GROAN . . .
Good morning, sleepyhead!
The servant, Thrull, started talking, and I learned that Ghazt hadn't told me everything. In fact, he hadn't told me much of anything. He had left out the most important part . . . THE TOWER.
That was the final straw. It was a good thing I had the makings of a plan—because now, I was going to put it into play—without question . . .
!!
FUME
SHAKE
IF THE TAIL IS THE KEY TO GHAZT BUILDING HIS ARMY AND CONSTRUCTING THE TOWER, I WILL HELP YOU RETRIEVE IT. FOR GHAZT. FOR REZZOCH.
BUT FIRST, WE MUST DEAL WITH THESE LITTLE HUMANS. . . .

Ugh. That awful mosquito-grade annoyance, Jack Sullivan, was there! Along with his little misfit band of apocalyptic wannabe heroes!
BOOM!
I watched, in awe, as Thrull unleashed a massive drill-bit creature upon them. I had never seen so much raw power.
Wow! You're the real Spider-Man here.
SCUTTLE
EVIE SNARK, IS IT? COME— TOGETHER, WE WILL FIND GHAZT'S TAIL. AND RECLAIM IT.
So you've tangled with the four little bratwursts before?
INDEED. IT WAS THEIR ACTIONS—ALONG WITH A WEAK-MINDED, SOFT-BELLIED CREATURE NAMED BARDLE—THAT PUT ME DOWN HERE.
MIDDLE SCHOOLERS ARE THE WORST...

I was overjoyed. We were about to get the tail. . . .
Shimmy, shimmy, cocoa pop. Shimmy, shimmy, rock. Shimmy, shimmy . . .
STRUT
Dandy-Lions
I thought we were going to fix everything. But instead, everything was about to go very, very wrong.
We're gonna get the taaaaiiLL! We're gonna get the taaaaiiLL!
If I had known what was about to happen, I honestly don't know what I would have done . . .
It was what happened next that changed everything. For Ghazt. And for me . . .

I couldn't believe what my eyes were seeing.
No . . .
Duped and deceived! By a double-crossing cosmic crumb bun!
Thrull would destroy Jack and his friends next. I didn't want to stay and watch. So I left . . .
I walked for hours. Rain came in buckets. I was glad for it—the way the outside world perfectly matched what I felt on the inside . . .

WHAT TOOK YOU SO LONG! WITHOUT YOU TO HOLD AN UMBRELLA OVER MY HEAD, I WAS FORCED TO COWER UNDER HERE LIKE SOME SORT OF . . . RODENT!
The creature woke up. His name is Thrull.

WAIT! WHAT?! YES! THRULL WILL HELP ME GET MY TAIL BACK!
Actually, he won't. He stole the tail. It's, like, part of him now.
EXQUEESE ME? BACON POWDER?
Don't say that. I say that. It sounds weird when you say it.
BUT . . . BUT . . . HE CAN'T! I AM HIGHER ON THE COSMIC POWER RANKINGS!
SMACK!
Guess ambition trumps status . . .
CHOC
SNACKIES

YOU HAD ONE JOB!
First of all, it was your idea to go get his help. Your buddy betrayed us. And more important that any of that . . .
What is the Tower?
WHAT? WHERE DID YOU HEAR . . . ? UM. OH, YEAH . . . RIGHT . . . OK, WELL . . . THE TOWER.
Yeah, the Tower. Forgot to mention that, didn't ya?
Time to spill the cheese!
IT'S JUST A LITTLE TINY THING. IT'S NOT IMPORTANT. IT'S A LITTLE TOWER. NOT EVEN VERY TALL. LIKE A SANDCASTLE.
CAN YOU TELL I AM LYING?
Can you tell I'm wearing glasses?
(I am.)

OK, LOOK. IT WASN'T LIKE I WAS BUILDING THE TOWER BEHIND YOUR BACK.
I JUST DIDN'T WANT TO DO IT, OK? THIS RAT FORM TRANSFORMATION HAS BEEN DIFFICULT FOR ME. DO YOU HAVE ANY IDEA WHAT IT IS LIKE?
Dude, we've all been through tough times. The difference is, the Monster Apocalypse gave me motivation.
But you just lost yours completely.
UNBELIEVABLE! I summon a monstrous deity from another dimension to help me lead an army, and he ends up being the laziest, most good-for-nothing cosmic creature that ever existed!
I hitched my carriage to the wrong rat! I am OUTTA HERE.
WHAT?? WHERE ARE YOU GOING? I AM INJURED! YOU WOULD JUST LEAVE ME HERE??
Clearly, you're not serious about getting your power back.
And you're not serious about us being partners.
So yes. I would leave you here. And I am.

I raced through the streets. Leaving Ghazt had me feeling revitalized, rejuvenated. Because I knew I wouldn't be anyone's servant again.
Sid's
AUTO PARTS
I would rise on my own.

I returned to the ABC theatre. The place where all my big plans went wrong. Where Meathook fell.
BLOCK

Meathook had been powerful. We had been a good team.
SUCH A GOOD TEAM!

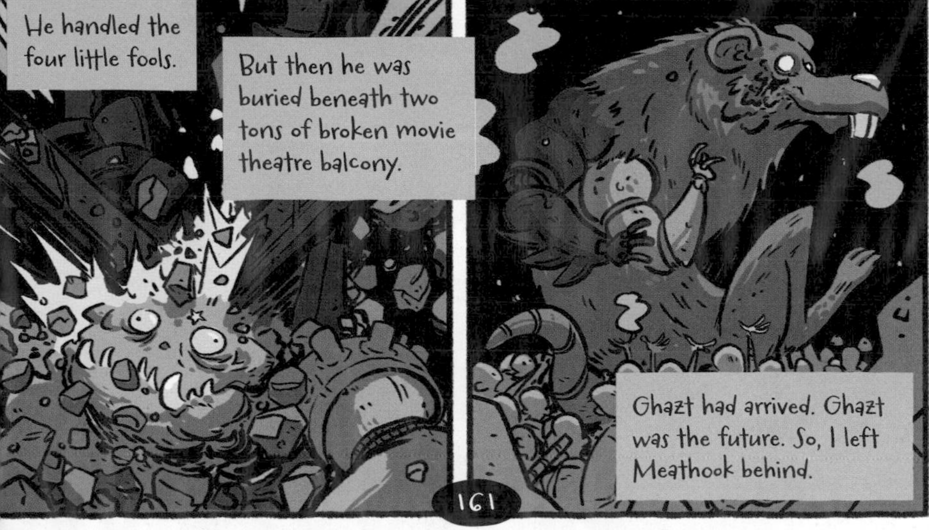
He handled the four little fools.
But then he was buried beneath two tons of broken movie theatre balcony.
Ghazt had arrived. Ghazt was the future. So, I left Meathook behind.

That was a jerk move, for sure. He had served me well. But I'd no longer had any need for him.

But I could make it up to him. By letting him serve me once again . . .

Ooh, Milk Duds.
MILKD

CRUNCH!
CLINK, CLINK . . .
Uh?
Something BIG was alive in the ABC Cinema . . . I hoped it was him . . .

My heart pounded as I entered the theatre—the place my life should have changed for the better. Instead of the opposite . . .

MURRRMMMM . . .
RAWRRRRNNN . . .

My heart vaulted into my throat.
Meathook! I'm coming!
Need a lever . . .
STAB!
Stupid . . .
super-heavy . . .
fancy . . . recline . . . seats . . .!

POP!
Meathook! We're reunited at last! We are—

RAWWWR!
OK, so you're a little angry!
SWIPE!
KRUNCH!

***AUTHOR'S NOTE:** That's Quint's fault! See *The Last Kids on Earth and the Cosmic Beyond.*

I would not allow myself to be manipulated again.
I would no longer count on anyone but myself— and my own plans.
wo Dozer spikes
19 meters of monstrous
1 Konag nail
11 strands of Rooket hair
Tongue of Tormensch
Each ingredient mashed, ground, brought to a boil— then delivered separately
I'll be back, Meathook. I will. Because...
I've got plans for us, big buddy.

I collected the ingredients. Quickly. And without any ... hesitation ...
Back at the RV park, Ghazt decided he was serious about getting back his tail—and his dignity . . .
WHO ARE YOU? GHAZT, THE GENERAL!
WHAT ARE YOU GONNA DO? GET STRONG AGAIN!
FASTER! STRONGER!
THRULL! I AM COMING FOR YOU!
Meanwhile, as Ghazt posed like Rocky . . .
I'd done it. I had found every ingredient!

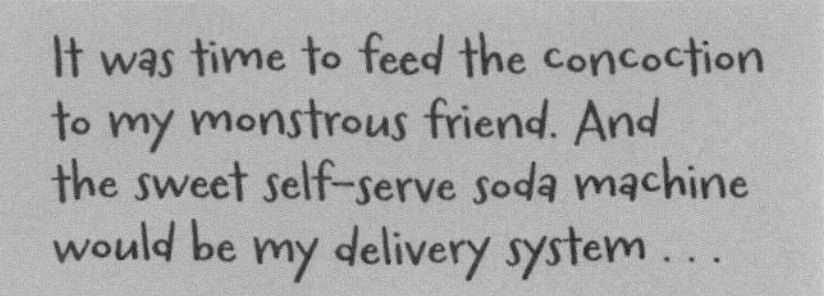

It was time to feed the concoction to my monstrous friend. And the sweet self-serve soda machine would be my delivery system . . .

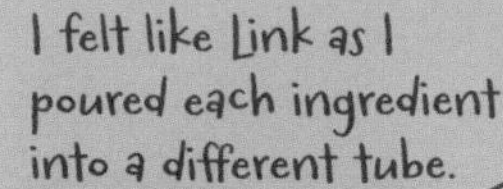

I felt like Link as I poured each ingredient into a different tube.

Double, double, toil and trouble. Bubble, bubble, Barnie Rubble!

Later . . .

Hey, Meathook! You're awake! Right on! If you had weird dreams about a bunch of tubes being hooked up to you— well, those weren't dreams.

You are going to love this. Each ingredient is connected to a different tube. And they all flow directly into you.

Soon, you'll be more than just a monstrous punching machine. You'll be **my** monstrous punching machine.

Now, how do you feel about a little hint of cherry vanilla? I'm a cherry vanilla gal, myself.

Here we go...
SLOOSH!
RUSHHH!
CONCOCTION INFUSION!
I have some things to attend to. But before I go, one quick thing...
RRRRRRUMBLE.
Not sure how long I'll be away, and I can't have you getting all superstrong and running off without me.
KICK!
CRUNCH!
Ciao!
What I had told Meathook was true—he would be more. But I left out the most important part: he would have to rely on me for his strength. That way—

—he'd never let me down . . .
WELL, WELL, WELL. LOOK WHO HAS RETURNED.
I HAVE RECOVERED. AND I AM STRONGER THAN EVER.
IT IS TIME I GET BACK MY TAIL, MY POWER SOURCE. I SHALL CRUSH THAT THRULL CRETIN FOR CROSSING ME.
Wow, I leave for a few days and you get your mojo back!

Anger has you focused up, huh?
Or wait. Is it something else . . . ?
You're scared! That's it. You're afraid! Because . . .
because if Thrull builds the Tower, then Rezzoch will come.
And he'll be super angry at you! Because Thrull will have done what you failed to do.

YOU SEE MORE THAN I REALIZED.

TAP TAP TAP
What can I say? Thick lenses.

I WANT TO STOP THRULL AND GET EVEN. IT IS AS SIMPLE AS THAT. NOW, LET US LEAVE.
Weeks earlier, I would have been ecstatic to set out on an epic adventure-quest with Ghazt, the great Cosmic Terror.
Just imagining it would have made me smile . . .
But now I recoiled at the thought. I would ride shotgun to no one.
If we're gonna do this together, I've got a few rules.
First, no more lies. Second, I am not your errand girl. We're partners.
And Third, you pull me on our journey. In . . .
WHIP!
THIS!
WHAT IS THAT?
It's my chariot. Like in Ben-Hur. It's supercool and you're probably jealous.

IT'S NOT SUPERCOOL. I'M NOT JEALOUS. AND I WILL NOT PULL YOU.
You will. You OWE ME.
I DON'T–
You know what will happen to you out there? A Cosmic Terror with no power?
In a world you don't know or understand? Picture it:
LARGE FIBREGLASS HUMAN!
I TOOK A WRONG TURN BACK AT AN EXXON STATION AND HAVE BEEN WANDERIN LOST FOR MANY DAYS. I NEED LIQUID CHEESE. PLEASE . . .
THAT IS NOT LIKELY! HOWEVER– YOUR POINT IS TAKEN . . .
So . . . PARTNERS?
PARTNERS.

And so, we set out as a duo . . .
TRUNDLE
I was OK with this now. But I promised myself, and I knew . . .
I would never be without a backup plan again.
BLOCK
I threw a glance at the theatre. I could almost hear the soda-serum machine inside—pumping, pumping, pumping . . .
I'LL be back for you, Meathook. I don't know how, exactly, but I wiLL . . .

I CAN SENSE THE TOWER. IT IS MINE. MY WEAPON. IT CALLS TO ME . . .
CRUNCH CRUNCH
CRUNCH. CRUNCH
Do you hear that? Sounds like footsteps. Weird, different footsteps.
?
I glanced to the side—and gasped at what I saw . . .
HIDE!
THEY'RE HEADING IN THE DIRECTION OF THE TOWER.
NO BOTHER, WE WILL GO AROUND THEM.
I don't think so. There's more. A lot more. Look . . .

We gotta move! Quickly—my chariot. That way!
Later . . .
What the heck were those?
EEK!
THE CREATURES AREN'T FROM MY DIMENSION.
HOWEVER . . .
THEIR ENERGY IS FAMILIAR. I FELT IT—IN MY WHISKERS. I DON'T KNOW WHAT IT MEANS. EXCEPT THAT WE SHOULD HURRY.
Hurry WHERE? We had only a vague sense of direction—and that got derailed pretty quickly.
I WILL LEAD US THERE. YOU MUST TRUST ME.
I do trust you. But I don't want to get there like thirteen years from now.
I WILL FIND US A WAY THROUGH.

Days later . . .
WE GO THROUGH THAT.
An old highway tunnel? Great, you know how I love being underground . . .
You know—you need to figure out a way for your brain GPS to take us on less dangerous paths.
TAP TAP
MY BRAIN NAVIGATION IS SUPERIOR. DO NOT DISRESPECT IT.
CLICK!
TRIP!
SPIKE SPIRAL!
That's not gonna be good . . .

FOUL SPIKY FIEND!
PIERCE! SHATTER!
They're gonna pincushion us! We've gotta—
Ugh, I can't move.
I can't move and my chariot was destroyed!
WELL, AT LEAST SOMETHING GOOD CAME OF THIS . . .

HELLO! WELCOME!
And your GPS didn't see it coming, huh?
BLAST. IT'S A SKEWERBACK. THIS IS A COMMON SKEWERBACK TRAP.
MY CHILDREN HAVE BEEN WAITING SO LONG FOR ME TO CATCH A MEAL. THEY WILL BE SO EXCITED TO FEAST. BUT FIRST—THE SAUCE!
DON'T GO ANYWHERE!
Skewerback? Children? What is this?
A SKEWERBACK CAN REMOVE ITS SPIKES AND MANOEUVRE THEM INDEPENDENT OF ITS BODY.

IT'S HOW IT CATCHES ITS PREY.
THE MORE YOU SQUIRM, THE TIGHTER THEY POKE.
Well then . . . this stinks.
CURSE THIS STUPID RAT BODY!
Wait! Your stupid rat body! That's the answer! Rats are all flexible and junk!
HUH?
Ghazt, it's time to embrace your inner rat. And not just all the cheese eating. You can squeeze and wiggle through anything. So, go on—DO IT.
I WILL NOT. IT'S UNDIGNIFIED.

OKAAAAYYYY.
THE AU JUS IS SEASONED TO PERFECTION! WHO'S READY TO BE TONIGHT'S MAIN COURSE?? MY CHILDREN WILL BE READY TO DINE SOOOON!

FINE.

OOOH, WOW. LOOK AT THIS.

I'M SO BENDY!

I didn't see what happened next.
I just heard it.
The Skewerback's scream as it tried to scuttle away. Then a loud—KRAK!
Suddenly, the spikes retracted in one quick motion.
SMACK!
YOU HAVE MADE A GRAVE MISTAKE.
I AM SORRY! PLEASE! HAVE MERCY!

C'mon, let's go.

NO. I AM NOT DONE HERE. I AM A GREAT AND POWERFUL BEING. I CANNOT STAND FOR THIS SORT OF DISRESPECT.
GO.
YOU DO NOT WANT TO SEE THIS.

So, I walked out. And I heard the Skewerback howl as Ghazt showed it just how powerful he was—even without his tail.

You done?
YES. AND SO IS THE SKEWERBACK. BUT ITS CHILDREN—
You were saying about the children?
I WAS SAYING THEY'RE NOT DONE!
SKREEEEEEEE!

Ow! Hey!
OFF!
SKREEE-OWWWW.

UH-OH.
What?? What uh-oh???
AGAIN? REALLY?

KRUNCH!
KRUNCH!

FLICK

WHOA!

This is incredible.

QUICK! I NEED A DISGUISE! OR ALL WILL KNOW I AM GHAZT!

You don't need a disguise! You're a giant rat.
YES, BUT I EXUDE A CERTAIN COSMIC WARLORD MACHISMO THAT WILL MAKE ME INSTANTLY DETECTABLE TO THESE CREATURES.

HEY! GET A LOAD OF THE SIZE OF THIS GIANT CHEESE RAT!
WILL THE PARADE OF EMBARRASSMENT AND SHAME NEVER CEASE?

Actually, that could be a problem. Thrull knows you've taken on the form of a giant rat, and he knows you're with me.
If we have any shot at getting your tail back, we need to get to the Tower without Thrull knowing.

Moments later . . .
BETTER?

Sure.

Maybe we can get on this thing— and use it to get us to the Tower.
ENTRY
WELCOME BACK! Would you like to pose for a quick photo to commemorate today's excursion to–
Oh my!
A HUMAN! How wonderful! You are only the second–no, third, no... fifth! Yes, the fifth human that I've encountered.
And you are quite small for a rat– but very cute!

So, what is this thing?
A Mælûsqçât. The largest creature I've ever encountered!

SNIIFF SNIFF
GASP!

SNIFF
SNIFF
SNIFF
SNIFF SNIFF
MMMM . . . I'LL BE INSIDE.
FLOAT!

Tell me—is there any way to direct the creature?
Not really . . . It appears impossible to control this great beast.
However, it does seem to sense when a monster is in great pain . . .

And it will seek that monster out and allow it safe passage.
Ya don't say . . .
RUMBLE!
THOOM!
Soon, Meathook. Soon . . .
THOOM!
RUMBLE!
HOOOOWWLLLL!
BLOCK
ASHER
OOH! SETUP FOR BOOK SEVEN!

Acknowledgments

THIS BOOK WAS a team effort—more than any other Last Kids book—and I'm thankful to so many people. Douglas Holgate—the man with the million-dollar hips (again). Dana Leydig, for endless help and guidance. Jim Hoover, for seeing this thing, getting it, understanding it, and guiding it. Leila Sales, for jumping in at the last minute. All the incredible illustrators who made this work: Lorena Alvarez Gómez, Xavier Bonet, Jay Cooper, Christopher Mitten, and Anoosha Syed. Josh Pruett, for so much. Jennifer Dee, for making so much happen during a time when making things happen seemed impossible. And my endless thanks to Abigail Powers, Janet B. Pascal, Krista Ahlberg, Marinda Valenti, Emily Romero, Elyse Marshall, Carmela Iaria, Christina Colangelo, Felicity Vallence, Sarah Moses, Kara Brammer, Alex Garber, Lauren Festa, Michael Hetrick, Kim Ryan, Helen Boomer, and everyone in PYR Sales and PYR Audio. Ken Wright, more than ever. Dan Lazar, Cecilia de la Campa, Torie Doherty-Munro, and everyone at Writers House.

© Ruby Brallier

MAX BRALLIER!

is a *New York Times*, *USA Today*, and *Wall Street Journal* bestselling author. His books and series include The Last Kids on Earth, Eerie Elementary, Mister Shivers, Can YOU Survive the Zombie Apocalypse?, and Galactic Hot Dogs. He is a writer and producer for Netflix's Emmy-award-winning adaptation of The Last Kids on Earth. Max lives in Los Angeles with his wife and daughter. Visit him at MaxBrallier.com.

The author building his own tree house as a kiddo.

DOUGLAS HOLGATE!

is the illustrator of the *New York Times* bestselling series, The Last Kids on Earth (now also an Emmy-winning Netflix animated series) and the co-creator and illustrator of the graphic novel *Clem Hetherington and the Ironwood Race* for Scholastic Graphix.

He has worked for the last twenty years making books and comics for publishers around the world from his garage in Melbourne, Australia. He lives with his family (and a large fat dog that could possibly be part polar bear) in the Australian bush on five acres surrounded by eighty-million-year-old volcanic boulders.

Big Mama visited the Penguin offices once.

Lorena Alvarez Gómez was born and raised in Bogotá, and studied graphic design and arts at the Universidad Nacional de Colombia. She has illustrated for children's books, independent publications, advertising, and fashion magazines. You can visit her at lorenaalvarez.com and follow her on Twitter @ArtichokeKid.

Xavier Bonet is an illustrator and a comic book artist who lives in Barcelona with his wife and two children. He has illustrated a number of middle grade books, including two in the Thrifty Guide series by Jonathan Stokes and Michael Dahl's Really Scary Stories series. He loves all things retro, video games, and Japanese food, but above all, spending time with his family. Visit him at xavierbonet.net and follow him on Twitter and Instagram @xbonetp.

Jay Cooper is a graphic designer of books and theatrical advertising (he's still baffled by the fact that he's worked on more than one hundred Broadway musicals and plays). However, nothing makes him happier than writing and illustrating stories for kids. He is the author/illustrator of the Spy Next Door series and the Pepper Party series from Scholastic Press, as well as the illustrator of *Food Trucks!*, *Delivery Trucks!*, and the Bots series from Simon & Schuster. He lives with his wife and children in Maplewood, New Jersey. Visit him at jaycooperbooks.com and follow him on Twitter @jaycooperart.

Christopher Mitten is originally from the cow-dappled expanse of southern Wisconsin, but he now spends his time roaming the misty wilds of suburban Chicago, drawing little people in little boxes.

Among others, Christopher has contributed work for Dark Horse, DC Comics, Oni Press, Vertigo, Image Comics, Marvel Comics, IDW, Black Mask, Gallery Books, Titan Comics, 44FLOOD, and Simon & Schuster. He can be found on Instagram and Twitter @Chris_Mitten and on his site, christophermitten.com

Anoosha Syed is a Pakistani-Canadian illustrator and character designer for animation. She is the illustrator of APALA Honor Book *Bilal Cooks Daal* by Aisha Saeed, *I Am Perfectly Designed* by Karamo Brown and Jason Rachel Brown, and many more. Some of her past clients also include Google, Netflix, Dreamworks TV, and Disney Jr. In her spare time, Anoosha hosts a YouTube channel focusing on art education. Anoosha has a passion for creating charming characters with an emphasis on diversity and inclusion. She lives in Toronto with her husband. Visit her online at anooshasyed.com and on Twitter and Instagram @foxville_art.

THE MONSTER-BATTLING FUN DOESN'T STOP HERE!

TheLastKidsOnEarth.com

Check out more books in the bestselling

THE LAST KIDS ON EARTH SERIES!

Jack Sullivan, June Del Toro, Quint Baker, Dirk Savage, Rover, and a whole bunch of monsters will return in book seven . . . COMING SOON!

Does **anyone** ever even look at the back endpapers?

Probably not.